The
We Ate Off
the China

❦

Devin Jacobsen

Sagging Meniscus

Versions of these stories have appeared in *The Nonconformist, Consequence, The Saturday Evening Post, BULL, The Summerset Review, Vol. 1 Brooklyn, Exacting Clam, Dead Mule, Beloit Fiction Journal, Adelaide,* and *The Chaffin Journal.*

© 2024 by Devin Jacobsen

All Rights Reserved.

Set in Minion with LaTeX.

ISBN: 978-1-963846-19-5 (paperback)
ISBN: 978-1-963846-20-1 (ebook)
Library of Congress Control Number: 2024944321

Sagging Meniscus Press
Montclair, New Jersey
saggingmeniscus.com

�

Contents

Possum on the Roof	1
The Man in the Sky	17
Secret Anna	26
St. Petersburg	36
The Good Life	55
The Summer We Ate Off the China	72
Bob	88
Tauroctony	109
Dagonet	121
Evil in the Object	140
The Elegance of Simplicity	148
Let Dogs Delight	171
Hitler in Love	184

The Summer We Ate Off the China

Possum on the Roof

When Mama died last fall Velvet would come in and read until I fell asleep, that is, until she started seeing JC. And it was JC who gave me Buttons, until the men from the animal hospital came and took him one day while I was away at school. Daddy says he thinks it was Pastor Jim who told them to come take Buttons, but all Pastor Jim wanted to know was why we hadn't been going to church since Mama died.

"I just do not get," says Daddy, raising up from his tray of food, "what kind of man takes another man's dog? Something there ain't right."

"I miss old Buttons."

"Buttons smelled like turd!" Dawn hollers.

"That's cause you girls never washed him," says Daddy. He was winking at JC, and JC blushed, but also nodding, the way he does whenever Daddy makes him shake hands.

"I'da bathed Buttons if I coulda got him up," says Velvet. "Even JC couldn't lift him on his own."

"He snapped once at JC!" says Dawn.

"Old Buttons," Daddy sighs, "he was too good for this world."

"I was just trying to get him to take his business outside," says JC, smiling from the one side of his mouth, smiling at no one. "But Buttons wouldn't budge."

"There's still that stain on the floor, where he used to lie."

"I musta scrubbed at it a hundred times," says Velvet, "and it still stinks like something awful."

"It smells like fish farts!" shouts Dawn.

All of us laugh except Velvet, whose mouth and eyes bug out. She and Dawn musta fought a hundred times because of old JC.

"Why I'll have you know there ain't no such thing."

"Ain't no such thing as what?"

"As fish farts, dummy. Fish ain't got but just one hole where they do all their business."

"Say what?" says JC.

"Now there's one for the quiz bowl. Tell me what's the name the hole they got?" says Daddy. Velvet is studying for the state quiz bowl. If she and her team can make it to the finals, she'll get a scholarship that will let her go to the capital for school for just the price of a bus ride.

"He was too good for this world," says Daddy, "old Buttons."

At that a clabbering comes over our heads. From the chair and couch all of us watch it, following that noise until one by one we stop chewing. The noise goes a-brushing and a-scraping and a-shuffling from one end of the house to the other, from the kitchen off toward Daddy's room. The noise is as close as it can be, coming from inside instead of out.

"Please don't say it's a ghost!" says Dawn. "I'm terrified of ghosts. I hate ghosts, no!"

"Why maybe it's the ghost of Buttons," says JC, smiling. He's telling it to no one, but he's telling it to Dawn. "Old Buttons is coming back from the dead to stop your gibing."

"Save me! Save me, JC!" screams Dawn. But Velvet is too busy thinking of what that word must be to give her anything but a look.

"It's that damn possum on the roof," says Daddy, his mouth chock-full with food. "One of these days I'm gonna stay home and shoot me that bugger. I got my .12 gauge pumped and loaded." He pretends he's sighting him through the roof. "Pshew! Goodbye, Mr. Possum."

"Cloaca!" says Velvet. "That's it! That's the word I was looking for!"

Daddy glances at my plate. "How come you ain't eating them green beans?" There ain't nothing on my plate but green beans. "Them's the stuff that's nourishing. Make you grow up big and strong."

"The word for what?"

"For what fish tend to their business through."

"Speaking of business," says Daddy—he wiggles the table from the couch so he can stand up, scratch his belly, and groan—"I gotta get me off to work. And these little varmints gotta get off to bed." Daddy's eyes are small from sleeping or too much food; it makes him hover over JC like a moccasin waiting to pounce, like he's something dangerous.

"Yeah, I guess I do ought to get on going myself," says JC, who wiggles his table at the far end of the couch. Daddy sits between them whenever JC comes over to visit Velvet. "I know Velvet's got more studying. See you later, Velvet—I mean, tomorrow at school." He waves to Velvet, then to the rest of us.

"Come back, JC!" says Dawn. "Don't be no stranger!"

At the door he and Daddy shake hands like they were proud of just being men, like something that allowed them to knowing a handshake for a club, though JC always shakes hands like he's a little confused. Daddy gives him a thud on the back as JC walks out to the dark.

"You ever joining the army, JC?" we hear Daddy asking JC outside. "As I recall, you was saying something about how you was supposed to be shipped off sometime last month."

"Yes, sir, Mr. George. As soon as I get my wisdom teeth out, I aim to ship right off."

"Well, when's that gonna be?"

"About as soon as I get the funds, Mr. George."

"About as soon as you get the funds," says Daddy.

We hear the keys jingle in JC's hand and we hear the truck door open and we hear them keys slip in.

"I bet you must be excited about going there to the desert and protecting your country. Shooting you a lot of them towelheads."

"I'ma shoot me all the towelheads I can," says JC.

"What are tailheads?" I ask.

"Hush!" says Dawn.

The three of us on the couch listen to that old pickup of JC's rattle and cough and get to moving; we can't hear a word now that's been said. The truck drives down the road out the park and Daddy comes to the door, but not without glaring up.

"I don't see that damn possum!" he shouts into the dark, poking his head up at the roof. "Your days are numbered, Mr. Possum! I'll be coming for you with my shotgun."

By the time we hear Daddy leave for the plant Dawn and I are already in bed and Velvet is in the kitchen doing dishes. She is putting things away very quietly, and if her shadow didn't break the light under the door now and then, I'd say she weren't in the house.

"I miss old Buttons," I say to Dawn. She is lying on her back, still awake.

"Hush now. Buttons ain't never coming back, so hush."

"You think Miss Evelyn will come over this weekend?"

"I think JC'll come over ten times before Miss Evelyn comes over once," says Dawn.

"Daddy says Miss Evelyn's got a big real house. He said she's got a TV and a fireplace and a big old yard that goes down to a creek and in the yard's a doghouse. You think if we move in with Miss Evelyn, she'll let us go get Buttons?"

"Hush," says Dawn.

So I hush.

It was a while and then I was dreaming. Whenever the covers were lifted I was smelling a whiff of Dawn's feet, a whiff of that stink that smelled kind of musty but also a little bit sharp, like something dead was under the wall, and then when them covers went down I no longer smelled it so much, only if I breathed and really tried, I could catch a whiff of her feet, and then my dreams were running and going and the stink was the smell of a fat man. He was young but not so young it couldn't've took him some time to eat him all of that food, which is how come he got so fat. Watching him walk was something funny, and all of us laughed and laughed at the silly way he had of walking himself. He was just there skipping along and swaggering like he thought he wasn't so fat as he really was. Just a-skipping along and swaggering. He had a thin little kind of black mustache and a rose between his teeth like they do in the cartoons. Well, the reason he was skipping, the reason how come he was so durn smart, was because he was on his way to paying a call to the lady he was in love with! And once she opened the door the group of us saw she was the prettiest little lady that any of us ever laid eyes on; you could see why he'd been skipping. Then the pretty lady came out, right there on the step, and the fat man gave her a hug and a long smooch (the rose was gone from between his teeth, which meant he must have eaten it), and then all a sudden the fat man who'd been fat, he wasn't fat no more but skinny like the little lady he'd been hugging, only the little lady was fat as the fat man had been. He'd give her all his fat! And that little lady who'd got big, her face was round as pie and her titties were hanging off her like two big ham hocks. And the fat man who'd got little, he was smiling and still thinking he was so durn smart, and the little lady who'd got fat, she was smiling and something happy, and before you knew what they were smiling about she reacht up under her dress and pulled out a baby and plopped him on her titty. Then that little baby, the group of us watched him suck, and he was sucking something hard at that there titty, and the more he sucked and harder, the bigger he began to get while the fat lady began to shrink, and when he finished sucking the baby turned to a full-grown man. It was just the three of them there on the doorstep, pretty as a picture, and all of them skinny again and smiling, and then I awoke because I could feel Dawn awake beside me, though I couldn't smell her feet.

The light was on under the door, and Velvet wasn't in bed.

"What's that creaking noise?"

"Shh!" says Dawn. "It's just that possum on the roof!"

And somewhere in the sound came Velvet's whispering, "I ain't doing it without protection."

For a while the two of us listened to the noise—it sounded like the possum was out there scratching and using his claws to dig a great big hole up through the floor because there was something in there he needed to get at—Velvet's voice now and then crying out the way she does sometimes late at night when she thinks the rest of us are asleep, until the noise laid off, Velvet, the possum, and JC.

Next day on the bus, Seesaw told us we had a test that neither of us had studied for, so me, Eugene, Seesaw, and Margie decided we'd cut school, so we snuck off to the woods, where Seesaw built a fire and the four of us passed around a cigarette that Eugene had stole from his brother and took turns telling tales. Eugene told a story about a dog who'd come on his lawn, who his older brother shot from a point-blank range, and Seesaw said he'd shot an eight-point buck with his daddy over last Christmas. Then Margie told a story about a woman looking for work, and how she and her daddy had caught the woman dancing around buck naked on a cow trailer so they had to run her off. Then after Margie told the story, Margie and Eugene began to kiss, and Seesaw and me went off in the woods so they could be more private, and Seesaw asked if I wanted to kiss, and I said I guess I wouldn't mind trying it, so the two of us started to kiss, but the whole while I kept on thinking, wondering about Buttons, if the people at the hospital were helping him get better and if I should ask Daddy if we could go to church so Pastor Jim would tell us where that hospital was at so that maybe we might go get Buttons or check on how he was. Then Seesaw asked if I still wanted to kiss and I said I was done, and then I went around a bush to pee.

Around lunchtime I was awful hungry and I decided to go home. Neither Velvet or Dawn was there, only Daddy, who was sleeping in his room. There weren't nothing in the fridge or cupboard. I poked around until I found a can of lima beans, but I got tired of eating them after a couple bites.

Since Velvet was staying late to study for the quiz bowl, Dawn came home alone. She threw her pack down against the wall so that the princess plates rattled, hard enough to wake up Daddy.

"You're gonna get a whupping."

"How come you wasn't at school? Debbie said she heard you and Seesaw skipped with Nathan's little brother. You're the one's gonna get the whupping."

"I'll show you something if you swear you won't fudge on me."

"Swearing's wrong!" says Dawn. She was following me to the bathroom. "But maybe I might could promise."

There in the trash can, buried under some paper, was a long yellowish bag like a big balloon before blown up or one of them packets of milk with some milk left in the corners.

"Gimme that!" says Dawn, snatching it from out my hand. "That's not for little girls."

"What is it?"

"It ain't nothing," she says.

"I'ma go ask Daddy."

"Daddy don't know what it is. He dropped out the fourth grade and can't spell *depot* or your own name sometimes."

"I'ma go ask him all the same if you don't tell me, Dawn."

"It's a summons for minding your own business is what it is," says Dawn. She was fingering the packet with the tips of her fingers, her eyes gigantic and imagining, like she was hoping it might be full of milk or what was left of it hadn't gone bad. "But I'll tell you if you promise not to go telling the whole world. Not Velvet, not JC, not Daddy."

"I swear."

"It's a tool for measuring spit. You spit in the bag, and if it comes out a little, you know you're thirsty."

"I don't believe you."

"Well, believe me or not, little girl. You swore, so don't go asking what ain't is none of your business in the first place."

That night JC drove home Velvet, and since JC was planning on staying for dinner the two of us went to get dressed, but when Velvet saw there weren't any food she made JC drive her to go get groceries, and by the time they come back Daddy had already left for the plant. It was already way past bedtime by the time she took the pizzas out the oven.

"Don't tell Daddy JC was here this late," says Velvet once we was all alone on the couch, "or else JC won't be allowed to come back." JC was coming back from excusing himself. "I'll ask JC to bring us to the fair and give us a ride on the Ferris wheel if you all promise."

"On whose dime? On whose dime, Velvet?" says Dawn, and Velvet shot her a look that said she had better shut her mouth if she knew what was good for her. "Don't worry, JC. Your secret's safe with me." Dawn winked at JC as he sidled back on the couch. He was using Daddy's own pizza tray on top of the paper plates. JC blushed, kind of smiling, looking confused and a little afraid, the same way he does whenever Daddy makes him shake hands.

"Hey, JC," says Dawn. She ate all her food while JC was in the bathroom so he wouldn't have to hear how loud she is at chewing. "I was just wondering—do you know who the best hung man is in the entire world?"

Velvet sets down her pizza and is about to tear Dawn's head off from the neck.

"Dawn, I swear! You say one more word, you and your filthy brain, and I'll give you a hiding so hard you'll—"

"Jesus! That's Jesus hung on the cross! Did you think I was being dirty? I wasn't being dirty! I ain't nothing but pure of heart!"

JC is laughing so hard he may be choking on his food. I know I'm supposed to be laughing too, but I don't see what's so funny, but I go on and laugh anyway. Only Velvet looks like she wants to die, that is, die or maybe kill Dawn.

"That's pretty good," says JC. His cheeks are puffy, and what with his stubble, his skin might be a baby porcupine. He ain't looking at nobody in particular, just talking as he does from the one side of his mouth. "They teach you that at school?"

"We heard the possum on the roof last night," I tell him.

"Hush, Jorlene!" says Dawn.

"I know," says Velvet. "Remember, I was right here with you when we all heard him?"

"No, I'm talking later. Once we was in bed. Dawn and me—"

But Dawn gives me a good kick in the shins. "Ow!" There'll be a big old bruise there come tomorrow. I slap her across the jaw, and it takes JC both and Velvet tearing us apart and yelling before the two of us can hope to stop.

"You two ain't nothing but little varmints!" says Velvet. She is picking up a piece of pizza that got thrown over during the fight. "This the reason how come Miss Evelyn won't come over no more. Daddy says he's got to protect her from y'all's roughhousing. Now what's this about the possum?" She turns to me, staring me to the bone. I can feel Dawn's eyes burning, the hurt blood throbbing in my shins.

"Nothing," I go.

"You sure?"

"I heard that possum out here with y'all."

After spraying the carpet where it got the red stain, Velvet comes back, sitting between me and Dawn. I can tell Dawn is glad about getting to sit next to JC, even if she's ugly from crying.

"You know, it ain't even a possum—the critter up on the roof. Today we learnt at quiz bowl *possum* is all wrong. Everyone else, they got to say 'possum.' But they ain't such thing as possums in this part of the world."

With that Dawn makes us go to bed. Velvet says JC is going to leave as soon as he's through with helping with doing the dishes, even though we know he might stay till after we fall asleep, and sure enough while I'm brushing my teeth I nod off once or twice and hafta catch myself from falling into the sink. Dawn is already asleep—pretending to be—when I crawl in bed, and before I can think to smell her feet, I am out of this world we live in . . .

It's a house. I think, Miss Evelyn's. The roof is as tall as the rest of the house is by itself, and coming from the back, I hear a deep-sounding dog scampering around in the yard, the tags on his collar going *clink clink clink*, barking at us through the fence, barking because he's happy to see us visit him. I can tell he's shaggy and large. They's flowers by the door in tubs, and the smell of someone cooking is what makes me open the door. And inside I hear a noise. I have heard the noise of this noise before: it sounds like a million crickets all crammed in under one roof, the noise so loud it makes my head start spinning, and sure enough they are there in that big room, from one wall to the next. Not a space to move through or step in since they are piled up together, all on top another. But the noise, it ain't from crickets, but's the wailing and crying of babies. Babies more than a mind can count. Some of them babies older, and some of them babies younger. Some of them babies in bow ties, and some of them babies in glasses. Some of them babies with skirts and aprons on, and some of them fooling around. Babies being tended, and babies tending to. Babies of all sizes. I suppose it was a house just filled to the brim with babies. Babies of all sorts. And them babies was having babies, and them babies was having babies, and them babies, they was having babies too! There ain't nowhere in the world, I reckon, where they'd gotten together more babies.

Well, the next time we saw Miss Evelyn wasn't until next year, wasn't until the spring for Velvet's graduation, which was a downright shame since by the time she paid us a call I couldn't remember what that house that had all the babies inside looked like, so there was no way in the world I could remember to know about asking if hers looked like the same one in my dream or not. Velvet's team didn't make it to the finals, which meant there was no more getting a scholarship to go to school in the capital, which was also a crying shame since that night at dinner Miss Evelyn said she had good friends down there in the capital that Velvet coulda stayed with if she had just come up with the funds to pay tuition, which she couldn't have done anyway. By now I'd almost forgot about Buttons.

Velvet had just finished setting out dinner when Daddy awoke. Before he could hope to sit at his tray, though, Miss Evelyn held out her cheek, which was to say Daddy shouldn't even think about sitting down, not until he gave her a good smooch.

"Howdy, Mr. George," says JC.

"What you doing, JC? You protecting Miss Evelyn from the likes of these here varmints?"

JC blushes, not sure if or what he should answer.

"George, you ain't yet asked about Velvet's big day or offered your congratulations," says Miss Evelyn. "Velvet was at the head of her class and gave the most wonderful speech I ever heard at a high school."

"That a fact?" says Daddy; he is already good into his chicken.

"It ain't but something I wrote when y'all was away last week," says Velvet.

"Oo!" goes Dawn. After bending over, she sets down her chicken, because lately she can't hardly stand it whenever someone else is talking and's been wanting to hog the attention. She's now as big as JC!

"You ain't gonna eat them wings?" says Daddy, eyeballing the stuff on her plate, leaning over some in his chair.

"Oh, George, you ain't even ate all *your* chicken. Give the child some peace."

"I'm just making plans," says Daddy, justifying himself. His eyes are narrow from either being asleep or from filling himself with food. "A man's always got to be thinking on down the road. Ain't that right, JC?" The grease from the chicken makes his lips and chin look shiny, like he was putting on gloss while he was driving over a road with holes.

"It's a downright shame Velvet won't be going no more to the capital. Velvet and I were just saying she coulda stayed with some good friends of mine. The capital is just to die for in the spring! All the azaleas in bloom and honeysuckle. The governor's ball is something else. Did I ever tell you the lieutenant governor is my second cousin once removed? I coulda introduced y'all two."

"Oo!" goes Dawn again. Every now and then she runs off to go puke, but today she's just being ornery.

"I call dibs on this here drumstick," says Daddy. He reaches over a finger and touches the one he wants.

"Go on," says Dawn, "I don't care."

"You know big-city living works wonders on a young lady's form," says Miss Evelyn. "I know it certainly worked wonders on mine. I went down with the soles of my boots clapping on the sidewalk, and the very next week I was wearing fifty-dollar blue suede shoes. I thought I looked pretty smart."

"I got an uncle who lives in the capital," says JC. These days Daddy don't mind if he and Velvet sit side by side on the couch so long as nobody takes his tray. He says he likes having his space.

"Why that must be Lena!" yells Miss Evelyn. And at that all of us turn at once as if expecting to find a ghost, but before it can say "boo" or we can say "where?" Miss Evelyn raises a thick bright purple fingernail. "In that there picture! Why that's exactly the way I imagine her—pretty as a picture! And you," she says, turning and sizing me down, "you take right after her down to the freckle. You got the same sky-blue eyes as the color of that dress."

"Married in sky-blue silk the color of her eyes," says Daddy from under his chicken.

"Oo!" goes Dawn. The way she's always rubbing her belly makes me think she ate too much chocolate.

"Lord, child, just go excuse yourself." And to forget about Dawn being obnoxious, Miss Evelyn scratches the back of her neck and goes, "Speaking of marrying"—she ain't touched a lick of her corn or her baked chicken because at the party she ate too much cake—"I don't mean to seem like prying, but what's the reason how come you kids ain't tied the knot? When I was your age I'd already had my third bun in the oven. What, JC, you got cold feet?"

"No, ma'am," says JC. "I'm just still working out all my prospects. Looking on down the road. I suspect we'll like as tie the knot as soon as most folks," he speaks from the side of his mouth. For all the world he wouldn't look at nothing but that tray of food.

"JC's working on fixing up an old Mustang his buddy Fred sold him. We're gonna sell that Mustang to pay for the wedding and a down payment on a house," says Velvet. "What with me working nights at the ValueSave, it oughtn't to take but six more months."

"By house you mean a trailer?" says Miss Evelyn. She's poking her chicken to test whether the meat's still warm.

"You can't get married!" goes Dawn. All of us stop our chewing from how loud she yelled. "You can't get married cause JC's already mine! I'm gonna have his baby!"

Daddy swallows whatever he's got left in his mouth, then stops. JC, who is looking down at his lap, smiles as if trying to keep himself from telling Dawn how crazy she is. Miss Evelyn scratches the bite she got on her neck. Only Velvet is seeming like she's ready to go off, like those seconds when the fuse of a Black Cats is lit and you're clenching to try and prepare yourself for the bang. But it is Miss Evelyn who says, "Hush, child. Being jealous is the Lord's foreworst sin. It ain't right to covet what ain't yours."

"It ain't that I'm being jealous; I'm just telling y'all all the truth! If anyone should be jealous, it's her should be jealous of me!"

"Dawn, you shut up!" says Velvet. JC goes on staring at his lap, smiling that smile, like there was someone down there telling him funny jokes that if he laughed at he'd lose a bet.

"All right," says Daddy. "Dawn, you mind yourself. Let's don't be messing with your big sister on her big day."

"She ain't the one that's big! I'm big!" says Dawn, and up she stands and shows us that big belly of hers that is not so fat now come to look at it but pregnant. "JC done knocked me up!"

All of us are looking at JC, daring him to tell us it ain't so, specially Daddy. But old JC just keeps on grinning, sort of rocking himself, still trying to keep himself from going off, laughing, losing the bet, until finally he says out the side of his mouth, "Nuh huh, Dawn. You're crazy."

"That's a fact," says Daddy.

"I never touched her, Mr. George."

"He ain't touched her with no ten-foot pole!" says Velvet.

"He ain't maybe touched me," goes Dawn, "but JC good as give me his seed, and I'ma have me my and JC's baby." Not one of us is chewing or thinking about dinner, not even Daddy. "I found me one of them bags. It was thrown away in the bathroom."

At that Daddy wiggles out from under his table and trudges back toward the bathroom to take a look, all of us watching him, watching Dawn, watching JC, all of us waiting to see if he will come back with some kind of proof to show Dawn she doesn't know what she's talking about, but it is not the trash can in his hand he comes back with but his shotgun, and before the group of us has time to wonder if he is bringing it out as a present, as some kind of prize for all of Dawn's craziness, JC is plumb out the door and Daddy behind him. Miss Evelyn screams. Somewhere in the night there's a shot.

Velvet springs up from the couch to try and stop him. All of us is out the door running after.

"Run, JC!"

That old pickup of JC's rattles and comes to life, and a blast of Daddy's shot strikes somewhere off the tailboard as the last of the bang dies at the moon. All of us, except Dawn, are out there standing amongst the trees, all of us watching the taillights of JC's Ford grow smaller as he hurries away from the park. The light from inside the house is too bright to be looked at on directly. Then all a sudden a scraping sound and rattling starts making its way from one end of the roof toward the other—Daddy is still holding up his shotgun, the smell of the shots still burning the hairs in our nose, and only once it draws close does he turn from staring after JC—to a sweet gum by Daddy's room and scrambles down the bark.

"It's that damn possum on the roof!"

The Man in the Sky

RIGHT ON CUE the four twenty-four from Washington was heard coming through the water and once it pulled into the station then like clockwork out stepped the conductor, the porters, and the whole confused mass of them blundering to find the way out. It had rained mightily the night before and all morning and all through the afternoon the sky had gained in gray for tonight an equivalent-looking storm, under the augurs of which the porters now were fighting over who could lay claim to the few places where they could set down luggage and hope to make a good tip. I watched him come out among the others and right as I saw him I thought, Now here is a fellow who doesn't know his crown from his fob, and watched him while he was handed a small valise and advance a few steps beyond the fray, open his watch, and stare up toward the mountain. He stood there a while, posed against it, still and peering up, as though it were it versus him, as though he hoped to see something that wasn't there or had been and probably would be again soon but he couldn't be sure exactly when that might be, and I thought, Maybe he knew the old master; maybe he's not only daffy but maybe he's been away from the continent for the last ten years or come back from a long vacation on Mars, so that before he started to set off toward the top there had been plenty of time to move forward and prepare to intervene. I had already glimpsed those outrageous boots, but what I had not seen was the gold of his chain, the brilliance of his spectacles, the fineness of his suit, and the cleanliness of his chin. My task was simple: simply to make him turn the other way.

"Welcome to town, good master. Please allow me to carry your bag," I was just on the point of saying; however, that moment he broke from his trance and turned and I at once realized my mistake.

"You're Rex Faucet," he said in that smooth and icy baritone that sounded like he was sliding you across a frozen-over lake, so that it was unclear whether he was pleased to see me or stating a fact. "Of course I've known you since before you were born."

"So much for the Sumner Bill," I remarked, "eh? What, didn't you read last month's papers?"

Come to find out he had not been back since the day he had run away some seventeen years ago and in the interim, having harnessed his industry and *savoir-faire* to yield a judicious wealth, he had earned the right to be called Professor of Natural History there in Ohio after studying some time in Paris, where he had read the big-sounding names—Lavoisier and Cheselden and Musschenbroek and Fourcroy—many in the original French and as proof of his new breeding he offered to quote me the opening of John in Greek, which I promptly politely declined. He had come back to see about Kyland. Or what was left of it. I told him there was nothing. That any of the remnants of the estate could best be taken in in the hodgepodge of brick that was going into the shanties over at the other end of Main. For the first time I detected a chink in that frozen timbre. Really ain't there nothing? he seemed to say.

"There's nothing up there anymore. You can save yourself the backache."

A whistle blew; the train was leaving the station.

"And how's ab—and what about the old master?"

Forthwith I recited him the overworn tale of the dozens of the old master's slaves who had fled with the first flush at Manassas and the others who had followed suit, leaving only women and babes and the aged and infirm and cynics by the time of Petersburg, of the daughters auctioning piece by piece the property and chattels, such as the phaeton he had loved racing at breakneck speed to the rest of the county's peril and the collection of silver he had used for entertaining the countless nervous visitors to pay for the horsemeat he could not deign to kill himself, and finally of the death of the overseer, the news of which had reached us scarcely as an event but as history long made fact, and finally of the finale of the old master himself, how on hearing of Custer's advance he had sent them ahead (the daughters) to an aunt's or something's and on finding the front door wide open and inviting as a bride on the night of her wedding what they had found was the old man alone in his chair with a gash to the wrist and Sir Tim the bulldog, always his master's confidant, lapping the proffered wound.

That primped and steel expression and its features that just barely hindered him from passing looked wildly rather shocked, so downcast, he whom I remembered as a lad could speak brawls into being with the cast-down glove of a word, and for a moment I felt rather sorry for all that had transpired—even for the old master, who had taken me under his wing—if it might otherwise mean I could have known him in the way of a brother as I believed I deserved.

"Come, I'll bring you to Potiphar's. He, Sulky, and Aunt Octavia run a boarding house over on Water Street. The rates are really quite satisfactory."

As the two of us walked, circumnavigating puddles that, like crumbs of heaven, demonstrated a gray sky earnest for rain and skipping plank to plank where boards had been cast down over the churned-up mud, he questioned me as to who was still around, saying he had come back hoping to embrace his mother, that he had written her since the end of the war at least once every week, addressing his missives to Kyland, but he had heard nothing back—of course she didn't know how to read or write, though as an addendum he was always sure to include the directive to whomever might be the recipient to let him know by note that she was still all right, alive—but he had heard back nothing and so he had decided to come and see for himself. He told me about his wife, whom he did not specify by name or how near she was to the right color, and about his five children, whom he was teaching to speak fluent French, and of his office that looked down onto a manicured lawn and cloister and of his library and collection of artifacts that were supposed to rival the old master's, which I myself still distinctly could envisage, having spent hours perusing the shelves beneath his pinions, all the while stepping gingerly with his bag, this *chat botté* whom I had once watched bend a plow into a spear and threaten a greater rival, leading me to misdoubt my modified course of action and once again entertain the archetype of ushering him down an alley or idle lane suitable to a first-rate drubbing.

All across the boards, lying there crimped and drowned, were dozens of worms come up on account of the recent downpour and I wondered why always after a heavy rain news never got round the local avian communities about the feast that had been prepared for them gratis by Mother Nature.

On passing a haberdashery he excused himself before I could say anything and turned in the store through whose window I watched him select the two nearest sweaters and matching scarves of aquamarine and extend the cash from his billfold and when he came out, after a quick wipe of his boots, whose leather he had managed to keep remarkably intact, he showed me their soles on which was printed the inscription *F. Pinet, Paris*, telling me that they had been the first item of real luxury he had permitted himself to own, that they had cost him more than a month's pay as a waiter in the Faubourg Saint-Germain and he had coveted them not because of their design of embroidered acanthus trailing the velvet buttons but because he had imagined himself wearing them in just such a moment, for he had kept faith that one day on returning to Kyland he would don the boots as proof he had achieved what for so long seemed downright impossible. I watched him, this man who appraised himself no less than the height of the upper hunky, set down his valise and step into the necks of each of the sweaters and fold up the stomachs and tie the arms round his calves and cinch the scarves over them for good measure and it was lucky he had bought them when he had for the rest of the path was enmired in a deep vexsome sludge as we proceeded toward the boarding house, but not before pausing before Taurino's Clock & Timepiece, which I was curious to see whether he might observe.

At first he plodded right past with the sign in his periphery; then he turned back as though there had been some silent mistake, like when a watch may have stopped ticking and you stare at the hands for what feels like longer than a second just to be sure it has . . . not stopped ticking after all. In such manner he was reading the words. "Is that . . . ?" "The same. He took over the store from a brother-in-law." I watched him shake his head, as though somehow still amazed by the great changes that time brings about in the affairs and circumstances of life, as though he had still not yet come to realize that to exist is but to hopscotch from one disappointment to the next, even when things seem at their most blithe, so that I was moved to propose a sojourn to a certain house I had come to know of late rather well, which he promptly coolly declined, replying that he preferred to settle in after the journey and as he hoped to have a look around before dark and before his return the following morning, the introductions and arrangements for which I was glad to assist even if his reserved and dandified demeanor still struck me as a disappointment; notwithstanding, after having exchanged farewells and shaken hands, I was resolved anyway to follow him while he retraced the path to town, unsure how he intended to proceed with his inquiry and thinking the possibility of his exacting some bloody revenge on the fellow at whose hands had proved his humiliation and consequent escape not entirely out of the cards. And indeed I watched him turn into the store, but not before removing the makeshift sheaths from his boots. Thereupon I was left weighing my options: if in fact he had come not as he had said but to enact the murder of his former nemesis, barring the presence of an honest customer who might witness which of us had served to pull the trigger or braid the knife, who was to say that I myself would not be charged as his accomplice and my innocent curiosity become the source of my downfall, thereby making my present remoteness and sudden urge to affix an alibi all the more imperative. However, the man had really been something horrible. Although I myself had never spoken him a single word, I had heard more mouthfuls harangue his evil, more curses sable his name, than could fill a bible twice over and had seen and lived alongside the consequences and if pressed to render a judgment was forced to admit that my heart was still at intervals moist in recalling the tears of friends, so that my curiosity got the upper hand and I quietly slipped in behind. Neither turned since they were already well engaged and I listened to their exchange from behind the shelter of a grandfather clock of dazzling flame mahogany.

"—reckon you're one of them uppity half-breed Kylands."

"My name, good sir, is Professor Poseidon Kyland—that is, I am Professor of Natural—"

"You can be the King of Siam himself, and if you think you can come waltzing in—"

"—and will have you know I can read and speak several languages—"

"—you'll be feeling the force of the law—"

"—that I have connections with men of peerage in Edinburgh as well as Paris, and that the house I own is the third largest private residence in Clinton County. Moreover, and most importantly, I would like you to be aware that during the past decade my education has led me forth into a light of understanding such that a yokel as yourself can never hope to have conception, as might a worm the workings of a steam engine—"

"Why you little uppity . . . you uppity son of a—"

"—and therefore I couldn't give a damn what you happen to *think* about no—about anything whatsoever. In fact the only piece of information you might know that I take of especial relevance is whether you auctioned my mother, Alice Kyland, and if so then to whom and if so then where might be her whereabouts."

It was while overhearing their contention that I regretted my decision to tail him, that I realized no good would ever come from their having such a dispute other than a compounding of mutual flames, whose warmth, I believed, one could palpably sense despite the haven of my shelter and I was primed to reflect on the likeness of the two, meaning that hate, much like the configuring of a clock, was rarely self-setting but seemed always to receive its ignition from like hate, as in the lighting of fire from fire, just as each of those many timepieces surrounding us three had not kept time exclusively but had been equated clock by clock. It was too late for slipping away. Soon I heard the white man catching his breath.

"Mother, eh? 'Mother,' you says?"

"That's correct, my good sir: Alice Kyland—a woman of petite carriage, barely four and a half feet in height, nonetheless exceptionally very beautiful. In addition you might remember she had a rather distinctive birthmark not unlike the shape of the African continent on her forehead near the temple as well as a scar that extended from the left shoulder down to the el—"

"I never sold your lusty whore of a mother anywhere south of the Alleghenies, and if you open your mouth to let in another slandering wind I'll kill you where you stand," he asseverated. "You damn mulatto bastard. Odds says she left with those heap of other niggers after the man in that weird carriage come through the winter of sixty-three."

"What man? What carriage?" I heard him declaim.

"What carriage, eh? Why a 'drosky' is what he called it. Comes up racing one day through town, blowing a horn, telling them's in rags it's time to cast down their burdens. Telling them grab what they can and make themselves ready to fly. Was nothing could hold them back no more. How they was supposed to be five-fifths natural citizens. Riling them up till they was plumb near out their heads."

"But Alice Kyland, where would Alice Kyland have—"

"Followed him hooting and hollering, I reckon, just like the rest. Yep, I suspect she's long, long gone. All of them clapping their hands and singing behind that drosky like they was David behind the ark. Closest thing to mass insanity I ever did witness in my life. Why you could hear them fools for miles once they was out of sight. I bet they're dancing a different prizewalk these days. Bet they're singing a different tune now. I tried to tell them but they ain't wanted to listen. Told them fools in the streets: 'Have fun paying your taxes! Have fun putting bread on the table, finding clothes to set on your backs. Good luck building a fancy old house. Ain't that what y'all wanted? Ain't no one gonna bend over backwards to help y'all out of a bind no more. Not when you killed his brother. Not when you killed his son.' I tried to tell them for their own goods but they was too gone out their heads. I says, 'Good luck finding a job—now that you're saying you're like all the rest of us. Yeah, go on and grab you another load of them names that don't mean nothing. Good luck and good riddance. Hope y'all got you some friends in some mighty high places to help y'all out of a bind.'"

Later that night I heard him come up the stairs and open and shut his door and I heard the springs cry out on the cot and the wet boots drop to the floor. He had been out in the storm, wandering the town and going door to door, asking if anyone could offer a word regarding his mother's whereabouts and no one had known nothing. No one had known anything.

As I drifted off to sleep I imagined him lying there, thinking over what old Taurino had said. Imagined seeing her join the drosky's train seeping out of the mountains and into the valleys and wilderness and into that new life we imagined waiting around the bend, all of them clapping their hands and singing and shouting in tandem:

> *Man in the sky, man in the sky,*
> *Cast down your load, get ready to fly,*
> *Man in the sky, man in the sky.*

Secret Anna

For the last six months my son has had an imaginary friend he calls Secret Anna. They do everything together—she goes with him to school; she follows him to baseball; she even helps with homework. I know I should be happy. Six months ago he didn't have any friends, and now that he has Secret Anna, kids have started coming to the house—they've already met Secret Anna of course, but they wanted to see where she lives.

When this whole thing started, I did what any parent would do and I pretended I was happy to make Secret Anna's acquaintance.

"Where are Secret Anna's parents? They must be worried she's not home for supper."

"Secret Anna doesn't have parents," said Traxel. He had turned nine that very day, the day he came home carrying a tupperware container full of funfetti cupcakes, Secret Anna having apparently ridden the bus as well.

"She doesn't have parents? Then how did she get her name?"

"She did have parents," said Traxel. I watched him thinking it over, inventing her life on the spot. "But they forgot to bring her with them. And now she's here with us."

That night, after tucking Traxel and Secret Anna in bed, I looked into imaginary friends. Apparently nine is still a typical age to be having a made-up friend. Sometimes there are sixteen-year-olds who think they have made-up girlfriends. In rare instances, sometimes these friends follow you through life, though in less severe cases you only talk to yourself. There was a moment of outright panic when I imagined Traxel pushing a shopping cart full of trash and castaway tires down the side of the highway, conspiring with Secret Anna how they were going to blow up the insurance companies and beget a whole society of imaginary, made-up citizens, but then I told myself he was just going through a phase—this too shall pass, just like the one where he ate only SpaghettiOs, stuffing, and Bagel Bites, just like the one where he insisted on being called Edison—this is just something he has to go through to become a mature adult. And we've been stuck with Secret Anna ever since.

"How was school?" I say.

Tonight Traxel's new friend Jerome is joining us for dinner.

"Good," say both of them.

"Jerome scored a touchdown today at recess. He did his touchdown dance. Show her your touchdown dance, Jerome."

The child shimmies up and down in his seat like he is bowing and running at once, like he is doing some kind of rain dance, and Traxel watches Jerome with delight.

"Touchdown mambo, touchdown bongo," chants the child, a chant as much as a song.

I too am delighted. For a while it seemed like he'd never have any friends. I'd ask him what he did that day at school, and he'd say, "Nothing," and then I'd ask him who he saw, and he'd say, "Nobody," and then I'd ask him how he was feeling, and he'd say, "Okay," and that was the extent of our conversation for the first six months.

"Tell her what Secret Anna did today," says Jerome, abruptly halting his dance.

"What did Secret Anna do today?"

"She did," recollects Traxel, looking up from his corn on the cob (thankfully I have never had to set out a plate for Secret Anna; all that is required of me in my part of the charade is that I give her a goodnight kiss on her invisible forehead that lies next to his on the pillow and tell her to have a good day at school), "Secret Anna kicked Mrs. Hutchins!"

"She kicked her?"

Both boys giggle.

"Mrs. Hutchins tripped down the stairs, and it was because Secret Anna kicked her in her big old bohonkus," explains Jerome.

"It's not nice to laugh when people end up hurting themselves," I say. "Mrs. Hutchins could have twisted an ankle or broken a leg."

"Mrs. Hutchins was being a boo. She was saying Toby couldn't have recess, and then, when she walked us to PE, Secret Anna ran up behind her and kicked her in the heinie."

"Secret Anna's parents should have taught her better manners," I say. "She's lucky Mrs. Hutchins didn't put her in time-out."

"Secret Anna can do whatever she wants," says Traxel.

After Jerome's father takes home his son, Traxel and his stuff are spread out over the carpet so he can work on his homework. On his fingers he is counting out numbers, the words of which are whispered into the air, no more substantial than, say, a faint reunion of ghosts. I assume Secret Anna is somewhere near beside him.

"How's it going?"

"I'm almost finished."

I sit on the couch and try to remember how I told myself to begin.

"Are you somewhere where you can take a quick break?"

Traxel's baby blue eyes look up.

"Look," I start, "I want you to know how proud of you I am. You've been such a trooper this year about doing just what you're doing now. Your grades have really improved; you've made so many cool friends, like Jerome. I'm so happy you're finally making traction as Mommy's favorite young man."

He looks at me like he knows all this, like I am explaining to him how to tie his shoelaces or that cats' claws extend and retract.

"But I'm a little worried about Secret Anna." Now his face starts to fall. "I'm proud of her too, but . . . don't you think her parents are wondering where she is? She must miss playing with her toys."

"I told you: they left her."

"Okay, right. But doesn't she have an aunt or an uncle somewhere who is wondering what all's happened to her?"

He is staring at me as if he expects me to know the answer, as if the answer were as evident as Secret Anna is to a nine-year-old.

"Secret Anna is fine with us. Aren't you?" he turns and inquires, inquires of the air right beside him. Either Secret Anna is recounting her whole life's saga or Traxel assumes I must have heard the answer as well.

"Well, what did she say?"

"She said she wants to stay here forever."

That night I dream I am on a tropical island, where I have gone for the day on a date. Suddenly I remember Traxel, but then in a burst of relief I recall I have hired a sitter to stay with him, so it is okay I am on the island, okay I am on my date. The sea is surging limpid billows of clear and muddyless water, and the sky above me is blue and serene and pure. I am wearing my new bathing suit, and I am going for a swim, and the water feels warm and inviting, like something that has come out to play. I am floating on my back. When I open my eyes, I am in the arms of a beautiful man whose name, I know, is Handsome, and I realize we desperately want one another. I am in his arms; I am on his bed. His chest is a tan waxed triangle.

"What are you waiting for? Get over here, Handsome." Now he is sitting on the edge of the bed in the hotel, staring at his fluffy pink slippers, looking quiet and quite forlorn. "What is it?" Suddenly I remember Traxel: it is now almost nighttime; I have told the sitter I would bring her home by ten, which is far too soon for me to get back in time from Hawaii. "It's just that," says Handsome, his downcast handsome head in his downcast handsome hands, "I'm sad I'm not really real." I can feel my wonderful night of pleasure beginning to slip away—Traxel is waiting for me and the sitter—and I try to think of anything I can do to ensure it may last, if only another minute. "No," I say, "that's not true," no matter that I can feel the slightly upward tinge to my voice that reveals what I am saying is not true. "You're just really sad." "I'm sad because I'm not real." And when I go over to the edge of the bed to comfort him, to console his sinewy back, sure enough, on squeezing him, I squeeze until he disappears to a memory.

I wake up feeling frustrated and as sad as Handsome.

One afternoon Traxel and his friend Marvin are playing down by the creek, and I get a call from a neighbor, who tells me they are shouting the f-word, each shout louder than the one before until they end up screaming pure vowels.

"Thanks," I say. "I will deal with it."

I know for a fact that someone has written that word in concrete over there by the creek, which is where the boys must have discovered it.

When they come home an hour later, their rubber boots caked with mud and smelling of young-boy sweat, which is not so much repugnant, the way it will be once they go through puberty, as adorable and innocuous, like it was watching him do tae kwon do when he was six, I clear my throat and commence my speech.

"Boys, Mrs. Ellerby called and said you were shouting by the creek."

"Yeah," says Traxel, taking off his boots in front of the carpet. "We were shouting f—" And I hear my son say for the first time in my life the word of hip-hop songs and pornographers. All of me goes cold, but I know I cannot get angry at him for saying something he doesn't know is meant to be bad, know I must approach this coolheaded and calm.

"But you don't know what that word means, do you?"

Both boys shake their heads.

"Good. For the time being all you need to know is it's a very bad word. From now on if you say it, you'll be in a lot of trouble. Is that understood?"

Both boys nod their heads.

"Secret Anna taught it to us," says Marvin, and if he were my kid, if Traxel had said that, I would probably push back a little and tell him where he saw it was scrawled in the concrete by the creek, but because he is not my son, I am willing to let this pass. Then as they are debating whether to play in the den or the bedroom, Traxel says, "Secret Anna, she said you can't keep saying that!"

"Is she saying it still?" says Marvin, showing his big white teeth.

"It's all she's saying. I told her she has to stop, but she won't listen."

Traxel looks back, glancing at me in the corner, waiting to see what I'll say.

"Stop, Secret Anna. No, she said you have to quit saying that. Stop it. Stop it! STOP!"

"Hey!"

They both look back.

"Trax, you and Secret Anna are both going to get a long time-out. Now I don't want to hear that word from either of you. Is that understood?"

He says that he understands, and he and his friend run off to play in his bedroom, and as they scamper away, I hear Traxel, in a voice he thinks is beyond earshot, tell Marvin, "She still won't quit saying the bad word."

At dinner there is this weird tension. We sit and eat our Stouffer's lasagna and Green Giant green beans not with a silence oppressing the room but with the loud prevalence of the f-word, the echo of my son's cursing by the creek, still rippling through the air like a tide roaring and flowing, never to ebb. It is not as if they have murdered somebody and buried the body by the creek; there is no blood or sin on their hands, only the tossed milestone that a child is getting older; there will be other milestones, more prevalent and more sinister, in the process of time, I assure myself, and if I am not ready to confront them, I very well should be.

"Ms. Oliver, may I have some more lasagna, please?"

"Yes, of course."

I get up from my chair at the table with the boy's plate in my hand, go to the counter by the stove, cut another square of lasagna with the spatula, put it on the boy's plate, which I set on his alphabet placemat, and as I go to sit on my chair, I land flat on the ground on my rump. Above me, screened by the tablecloth, I hear their uproarious laughter. In that moment I was going to sit, those frail microseconds of the planned loss of control of a blind backward free fall, I assumed I would be caught by the seat of the chair, but I landed right my rump, landed on the hard tile floor. From now on I will be distrustful of sitting.

Having returned upright in my chair, the shock still smarting in my tailbone, I say: "There's your entertainment for the evening, free of charge."

"Secret Anna," says Traxel, "that was great."

"Huh?" I say. "What was that?"

"Secret Anna pulled the chair out from under you when you were going to sit."

"No," I stare at him until he finds me looking at him, "I missed the chair and I fell."

"Nuh uh. She pulled the chair out from under you. Secret Anna that was awesome!"

"Look!" I say, striking the table so that the silverware shudders in place. "Secret Anna isn't real! She doesn't exist! She's just a figment of your imagination. And if I hear one more word out of you about Secret Anna tonight, you'll be grounded for the rest of the week, is that clear?"

The way he is looking at me—shocked, effectively disappointed—I have hamstrung him in front of his friend—says he cannot believe me: either believe his made-up friend isn't really real or believe I want nothing to do with her, with him.

For the rest of the night, after we drop off Marvin at his house a few streets away, Traxel will not talk to me. He does his homework with the concentration of a tinker repairing a watch, and at my attempts to check in he either nods or shakes his head. Aloofness is his game. He is as silent as Secret Anna. I worry that, as a result of my slip, now his friends will all abandon him, that maybe it really was Secret Anna who was vital to his success, that soon will go the good grades, soon will dissolve that burst of brightness, this season of relief we have enjoyed. If Secret Anna was the price of Traxel's adjustment, could I really not afford paying her? Is my vanity really so fragile it could be shattered by a person who doesn't exist? When I go to kiss him goodnight, I kiss the spot where Secret Anna usually sleeps, but on my doing so he says, "No."

"What?"

"There's nobody there."

"Aw, honey," I say, stroking his hair, part of me recognizing that I am merely touching him in order to comfort myself that my son is no figment of my own imagination. "Look, I'm really—"

"Just go," he says. "Please."

What can I do but go?

The next day he and Jerome return together from school. I have made oatmeal-raisin cookies to help atone for last night's outburst, and when they smell what awaits them, they come scurrying to the counter. Jerome has eaten three before Traxel takes his first bite.

"How was you boys' day?"

"Okay," he shrugs, and soon the two of them are off down the driveway, Traxel on his bike, Jerome following on Traxel's skateboard. I do the dishes with the seriousness of a penitent monk, making sure every fleck of batter has been rinsed down the drain and that the bowl and sheets are pristine, shining. As I wash and dry, I think about whether there is any way I can convince him that Secret Anna truly exists. *"No, you see, just because she isn't physical, doesn't mean she has no bearing whatsoever on reality."* But I cannot think of a line of argument that doesn't sound overly contrived and like a theological discourse on a principle of grave contention, so I decide the best I can do is offer a heartfelt apology and the promise of a nice vacation for the two of us this summer after he finishes fourth grade.

When they return, there is mud on their sneakers that displays the reluctant fact they have been playing again by the creek. Jerome is proudly touting a skinned knee, and I go for the band-aids and disinfectant while the two of them take off their boots and discuss the differences between water snakes and moccasins. For the rest of the afternoon and then through dinner there is no reference to Secret Anna. No knowing glances or allusion that would suggest her presence about the table. Finally I cannot refrain from coming right out and asking: "Did you boys have fun today playing with Secret Anna?"

Both of them quit chewing. For a second they stare at me as though I were daffy, like I had told them underwear doubles as a nice hat or had posed the question in a foreign language.

"What? Isn't Secret Anna—"

"Secret Anna is dead," says Traxel. He pronounces the fact flatly, without expression, emotion, or narrative.

"What?" I say, unsure whether I want to have heard him correctly.

Jerome's mouth is partly open: I can glimpse the unchewed food that he has tasted but yet to swallow. Whether their seriousness is a matter of disinterest or grief at the loss of their friend lies beyond my ability to judge.

"But . . . how can . . . why did she die?"

"Secret Anna was hit by a bus," says Traxel, suddenly enlivening with enthusiasm.

"She was hit by a bus!" cries Jerome. "That's awesome!"

"Yeah!" says Traxel, envisioning what were the circumstances, what were the last moments of her unseen demise. "I told her she had to look whenever she's crossing the street—I told her she always had to look out both ways—but she never listened. She was crossing the street and WHAM! Secret Anna was hit by a bus."

"Hit by a bus!" sings Jerome. "Secret Anna was hit by a bus! Secret Anna's dead as a doornail!"

"As she was hit I heard her scream f—"

For that I have to send him to his room, but I do so, punish him, laughing. I'm glad Secret Anna found a nice way to die.

St. Petersburg

WE GOT THE LAST of the balloons and flowers all loaded that Donette insisted on bringing home with us, even if they were already looking pretty sorry, like they were withering and starting to die. It was a hot day for a wedding. So I got in and started the car and ran the AC a while before Donette got in with the baby. I've been in here so long it's gone to blowing only warm air. Donette will have something to say about that.

I don't know how many years I've sat round, waiting on Donette. I reckon I must have spent a third of my life sitting round, waiting. I've gotten real good at sitting. There were decades I thought barking would help move things along, but after a few more decades turned over, I learned there weren't nothing more to do but sit round and wait. There's God's time and Donette's time. Ain't no time in between.

"How come there's no cold air?" she says on opening the door, moving the box of candles on the floor so she can scoot the ice chest closer up toward the fan. She's holding Baby Henry in one arm and the ice chest in another. "Put it down on cold."

"It was on cold, but a car insists on moving if it wants to keep on blowing cold air."

"Well then let's get on the road. I told Val and Jeff we'd send photos of Henry asleep in the crib before they land."

With Val and Jeff on their way to the honeymoon, we're looking after the baby. When I was her age, I thought I was living the high life, going to Florida and staying at a friend of a friend's. These days kids ain't ever content unless there's a celebrity's been there or unless they can take a million photographs to post all over the internet.

We're almost at Houma and she's still going on about stuff we brought back from the wedding, the baby fussing, wanting his mama, sounding like a squeaky door creaking closed.

"You remember for Kate's we saved the top layer and then it melted right away? Well I talked to Liz and Liz told me she learned a good little trick where you wrap the cake up in saran wrap—you have to be okay with the icing not being so pretty when you open it up after defrosting everything—and then rather than put it directly on top the ice, where the cake'll get all melty, you set a layer of packing peanuts in between, and that way it stays cool and won't get melted on the ride home. Isn't that something? Hey," she starts, looking over. "How come you always munching? Always got that munching look going on?"

"Can't help it. It's something of a tic."

"Well cut that out. You look mad and a little bit touched. Doing that through the wedding. Lord have mercy, I hope you weren't making them funny faces through the photographer."

When we pull up into the driveway, Baby Henry is sound asleep, and Donette goes in to lay him in the crib while I unload the stuff for now in the kitchen.

"Here," she says, a bright light under my chin.

"What's that?"

"That's the ocean in Costa Rica. Val says the turbulence on the airplane gave her a migraine, but she took a few aspirins. Jeff had to carry her down to the beach."

"That old Jeff is sure gonna have his hands full from now on. He'll have to start feeding himself with his feet."

"Oh you just hush yourself, mister," she says. Soon she hollers out from the kitchen: "What you wanting for dinner? You feel like grilling some of this steak?"

"Honey," I says, "I just drove... drove... drove... drove..." The word keeps sticking against my tongue.

"All right, I'll go and fix it myself!"

Over dinner we're keep on interrupted by the news in Costa Rica.

"Look, that's them with coconut daiquiris. What's that you think on top, whip cream? Val says that's coconut-flavored ice cream. She says Jeff just had one sip and decided to order a beer."

"Uh huh." She fixes me with that stare that says it wants more than the minimum tribute. "Cute."

"'Cute' ain't the word for what that there is. That's what they call real romance. She says it's hot and Jeff's worn out and is wanting to go to bed, but Val won't let him. She's making them go to the fireworks show."

"I thought she had a migraine?"

"I guess she must be over that."

We're sitting around, the dishes rinsed, the balloons and flowers everywhere all over the kitchen, the cake put away in the freezer, Donette in her modal pj's, now and then hmphing over the phone, my ears still ringing with that accordion, the news on for just some old noise, and I've got me a bundle of Little Debbies I'm working my way through, when Donette says, unlooking up, "What you think about going on vacation over to Florida?"

"Say what? You mean right now?"

"We took the whole week off to be with Henry. When else we going some place until two years, once after you're retired? It's October and prices'll be real cheap. We'll leave first thing in the morning."

"There ain't—"

"I ain't asking you, Claude. Think, when's the last time we spent real time together *romancing*?"

"There ain't no room for any romancing with a baby crying every two minutes and diaper-changing by the side of the pool. Besides, you can't drive no baby ten hours to Florida."

"Don't talk drivel. It don't make no difference to him if he's in a car or in a playpen. Let's go. Let's take a honeymoon for ourselves, for old time's sake. Let's go to St. Petersburg like we used to. For old time's sake. Let's go."

Most days I have to sort of remind myself I pretty much take for a fact that Donette is a better person than me. She's got her eye out on living life like a good person—and not just regarding herself but looking out in most ways for all the rest of us. There'd be nights where I'd come home dog-tired from building all day and running around, and she'd force me into doing some board game or into some outing, which at the time I fought against wanting to do but now see the why and how come of it, why she done what she did, and I'm most grateful for it. She knows what she's doing. She always did.

"Well, if I do go, I'm set on bringing my golf clubs." Because after all I got to have me a little vacation if I'm on vacation.

"You just be careful you don't go hurting yourself. You ain't as young and fit as you used to be."

We left before dawn, only us awake and the frogs and crickets. The last thing we brought from the house was the baby, whining that he be left alone. I'd been up all night myself trying to get me some sleep. I can't remember the last time I got a good eight hours of solid night's sleep, nor what that done to me physically. I suppose it's like being in good health—you don't know what it was you lost until you don't have it no more. Now being awake all the time is just one of those things you do, like taking a stool softener four times a day.

In Mobile the rain starts coming down, big, thick, loud drops of it, so big I can hardly squint to make out the stripes down the road. "Didn't you bother checking the forecast?"

And soon enough the shower is pouring down on us, lightning every which way and corner. Baby Henry must sense our nerves are up and won't hush despite Donette's sweet-talking. So much rain there is everywhere swimming across the windows; it reminds me of one of them visual aids you see of all the sperms swimming off toward the egg. But as soon as we pass through the tunnel and are up out over the bay, the rain tapers off, and we pull over for Donette to change the diaper and for us to eat some breakfast up on the fort.

Back on the road, the baby is wide-awake and done fed up; he wants his mama, nothing else.

"Feed him a bottle."

"He just was fed a bottle, Claude."

"Well then try feeding him another."

But nothing will calm him down, keep him from squeaming, so Donette turns on the radio, searching for some music that may help to get him to hush.

> Well, she's my first wife (first wife!)
> Yeah, she's pretty good, but she ain't no second
> First wife (first wife!)

But all it is is just a bunch of old noise, noise in organization.

Finally we decide on the AM Bible show, Donette bouncing Henry upon her knee while the preacher in a low, deep tone reads out Scripture, talking about angels coming down from heaven with seven big bowls they gonna pour all over the face of the earth and wash away the sin like they done in the time of Noah, each of us listening, even Henry, who seems to understand all them words. I guess you could say I do and I don't. Now and then a fellow gets himself to thinking, which, I think, is a good thing. I believe He wrote the Good Book for a reason, and there weren't no reason to lie about none of it, but cut my corn if He didn't take such simple-sounding words and fill them up until He makes them so durn complicated ... and yet with the way folks get to talking like they were filling up a shaker of salt with salt or a shaker of pepper with pepper ... I spent years working on some of them words like cracking some kind of nut and still can't get to the flesh of them, words like *good, bad, evil, wicked*. Time and again you see folks speeding past, only eyes to get down that road, eager to tend to business, and you know there ain't nothing there at the end, that they're only gearing up to turn back around. I don't mean to question His wisdom, but in my sixty years on this earth I seen both good folks being evil and evil folks being good, and I'm mighty curious to know how the Lord determines in between. Most days I reckon it's just better to throw away them words like tools for a different trade—even sometimes *love* and *faith*—and do the best you can with the leftovers.

"You making that munching face again, Claude."

"I told you I'm just thinking."

When we're reaching close to St. Petersburg, we're greeted by a gridlock of honking and so many high-rises angling for a view you'd never know a beach lay around the corner if it weren't for the salt on the wind. Donette this whole time has been telling Baby Henry what's out the window he can't see: "There's the rain clouds we passed under." "We're coming out Pensacola." "That boat's washing up on the sand." When Donette and me first came here, there weren't nothing around but sand traps and a handful of bungalows. Now it's all rich folks moving down from the city, building condos where they can hibernate for the winter, hogging the view and raising the prices up on the rest of us. For years we were going to this place the Gulfside Inn, but once the girls were all grown up, we quit coming. Most trips these days are spent on seeing family.

"*Ooooo*, big old stretch!"

For the life of me my fingers won't quit jerking where I took the keys from out the ignition. About everything looks the same. Even though new high-rises are popping up everywhere, it's nice to know the Gulfside hasn't changed except the fresh coat of paint since I last seen it some fifteen, twenty years ago. Donette sets me down with Henry, and I'm doing the best I can to catch the door from closing, but that boy is pure deadweight.

"Hello," she says to the gal at the reception, both of them ticking their nails on the desk, in different places. Her hair's done up like a beehive on the flat side of her head and is the color of honey dripping down toast, and she don't pretend to wear the bare minimum amount of makeup. "We don't have us a reservation, but we're hoping to rent a room for six or so nights. Is Mr. Angus in?"

"Who?" says the little old gal.

"Why that would be Allen Angus. He was the general manager during the several years Claude and I have been coming here. This was probably before your time."

"Oh, yes, Allen Angus. No," says the girl. "I knew I heard of him, but I actually don't know him. I believe I remember hearing someone say he died some time ago of a stroke. That was at least four years ago. Did you all know him?"

"I see," says Donette, "I see."

"Would you like a one-bedroom room or a two?"

Inside the condo everything smells the same, looks the same, feels the same. You'd think I'd forgot, but I guess I didn't. They got these big glass bowls on the table filled up beyond the brim with seashells they found on the beach—I remember one time Kate stole one of them sand dollars that we found out about only once we got home and Donette made her mail it on back—and on the walls petrified starfish framing the mirrors. The whole place smells bright and clean and faintly of the ocean; that thick carpet everywhere reminds me of the kind Donette put on the rim of the toilet seat to make sure I keep on lifting it. I see to it that all the bags are brought in while she's still sitting on the sofa, bouncing Henry. "Now you the one that's scowling. What's eating on you?"

"I believe I'm getting a migraine. I believe I may go lay down for a while."

"Well I was wanting some food."

"You go get you some food. Just do me the favor of bringing the baby along with you."

Well, if that weren't for a woman! Drive me twelve hours across the country, she insists, and when she's there it's something else. She ain't had one of her sick headaches in fifteen-odd years, but what can a fellow do? It's like them boxers that get whupped upside the head so hard they can't do nothing no more but laugh.

So I take Henry with me to the grocery store; it's in the same place that it used to be, only the name's been completely changed—it used to be a Blair's or Bell's or something's—now it's a new Value-Save, and while me and Henry are scrounging for food, I can't help but think to recall about Daddy. Come this May it'll be forty-two years since he passed—that's two years older than me. Lord knows He didn't make it easy. Hollering and gibbering with that touched speech like a man gone out his wits. That year in bed. Spouting all kinds of nonsense like some obscene kind of baby. And screaming. Lord, that terrible screaming that kept us wide-awake. Pouring his meals ground up between his teeth, hoping a little bit might take. Poor Daddy. What'd that fellow think it was—Huntington's disease? Whatever the name, that don't make suffering that kind of pain easier. For, as they say, band-aids don't patch bullet holes. Poor old Daddy.

Donette's still laying in bed when we come home with the groceries. Laying there like something that's been washed up onto the sand.

"I fixed you a sandwich. Potato chips on ham." Only there in the dark she waves the plate good away.

After the crib is fixed up and Henry sound asleep and I relieve my sweet tooth with a helping of oatmeal pies, I go in there myself, not kidding myself I'll be able to sleep a wink but just doing it out of practice, hoping that the motions might mean maybe the same thing as effect. She's changed into her pj's, Donette has; her eyes are closed, but I can tell by the way she's breathing she's still awake, though only a fool would try and engage her and hope to back away unscathed. That long body rising and falling, getting bigger under the covers, then a little less big. There's something about another body lying round to make it known a man's alone. It's like that echo that comes from far off. You wouldn't have thought to even think about that echo if it hadn't echoed at you in the first place. And hers once just like Val's, and me once just like Jeff, just itching to get my hands all over it. She was fifteen when Donette first gave her the talk.

"And what about Daddy? He don't have one thing on his mind. Or else he couldn't do nothing."

"He did have one thing on his mind, at one point, yes, your daddy did. Your daddy's just like all men."

"Then how'd you know . . . ?"

"Then how'd I know then that he was the one? I guess I just kinda knew."

And them hardly caring one way or the other until they run it out of us and then us the same as them.

At one point in the night Baby Henry is up and crying, and I don't need the wrath of my beloved to go telling me twice he's awake. We go out into the den, then out onto the balcony, where I bounce him against my chest and say to him, "Now, now; now, now, little man," hoping that that sliding door is sound proof enough not to wake Donette. He's crying because he wants his mama: his diaper ain't wet. Then after a while he's only sniffling. He's just confused like all the rest of us. I feed him his bottle while we're sitting out on the chair, feeling the warmth of the salt sea breeze and hearing the surf and the cars not too far off. After I get through with burping him, he gives me this sleepy-eyed look. Sleepy but also alert, like the look of a captive animal. Who of us'll be the first to break his stare? It's enough to shake me to the core. Those pale little blue eyes, thin and also alert, nervous but know what they're saying, not stammering but insisting, insisting on their questions. I can read them in his eyes. It's as if he's saying, asking me: What am I to you, old man? Are you all that I have left? And I can't help but wonder whether a part of him will maybe remember this when he's an old man too.

Next morning we went out alone, Baby Henry and me.

"I don't guess you're feeling much better," I says, saying it from the looks of her.

"Take Henry with you when you go," she says just long enough to fix me with that stare that means nothing but only one thing. "And turn the air down, would you." Then she rolls back over, squeezes a pillow over her face.

I scratched my nose. Another night not sleeping a wink.

"Say what? You can't bring no baby with you on no golf course. They got rules and regulations. And spend five hours in the boiling sun where—"

From underneath the pillow: "You only playing nine holes these days anyway, Claude!"

She's got sharp eyes out, Donette. I swear I could have brought the fellow who invented the sport, as God as my witness, and Donette would have told him point-blank to his face he'd gotten it all wrong: "We're playing it now with a bat and wiffleball," and by golly he'd have to listen.

"You want what?" says the teller there at the clubhouse.

"The stroller, it's got a cover that comes down," I go, "see, so he won't be hurt by no stray balls or burnt by too much sun. It ain't my idea but you-can-guess-whose."

And them old boys in the lounge there grinning and snickering.

"Your tee time's in a quarter of an hour." He hands me the receipt. "Feel free to have a beer while you wait or an apple juice."

Sure enough, once we're out on the course, we're catching some funny looks.

"Y'all play through, play through," I wave them, everybody, on. "I got to change me a dirty diaper. A bowl of old monkey sausage."

"Are you improving your lie," says a fellow, "or just making matters worse on yourself?"

"Hawdy haw haw. Y'all boys have a nice day."

There was a time when I was close to hitting par. I even got invited to a few nice tournaments. I remember going out with these boys we were doing business with out to Pelican Point and hitting a hole in one onto the fifteenth green. Not an easy feat, if I do say so myself. And all them boys just standing around, slack-jawed. Then going and doing it again on the sixteenth. It was like I was Jesus walking on water. None of them boys could believe it, looked at me like I done that sort of thing every day of the week, like brushing my teeth. But golf ain't no blink-of-an-eye game, and there was always some work to be done around the house, some errand to run with the girls, and I suppose it just made sense not sticking with it the way I might have wanted.

Lining up on the fourth fairway, I suddenly feel myself sort of besotted and let go the iron, finding myself sitting over it spraddle-legged. My left foot twitching and jerking. Ain't nobody around to see or call the ambulance, which is lucky for me since it saves the whirlwind of trouble of explaining how to handle the kid and them working up Donette to take away my car keys and not liking herself to drive, but within about a minute I'm back up on my feet, only my left foot still is jerking, and of course a few minutes later I duff the shot.

When two years ago I had the accident, the doctor prescribed a bottle of oxycodone to take the sting out of my leg. I saved me most of that bottle, and it was then at that point I told myself, If you ever know for a fact you're going down the same road as him, if it's ever there right as rain round the corner, you take these right away. Don't you hesitate even a minute; nothing ain't worth that. There ain't no amount of days of living on this earth worth going through that kind of pain, and putting other folks through that kind of pain too. And they been hid in my drawer ever since.

"You taking him next to see the Dalí Museum?" says one fellow at the clubhouse. "Seems like you're endowing him with rather sophisticated tastes from a young age."

Back home Donette's still laid up in bed and fiddling over her phone. Even in the dark I can see where the tears have stained the pillow.

"How you been with that migraine, boo? Looks like you been up and about."

"I took me some Advil," and now she rolls over under the covers, "but I'm still under the weather. I just prefer to keep here in the dark and you and Henry use the living room. Val and Jeff've been texting all day. She says they're commencing to get heavy rains coming up toward Panama. They're keeping a close eye on everything. They're starting to close up the shops and stores."

"Panama's a long way over from Florida. Everyone can just cool it and hold their horses. The governor'll send word it's time to ev—"

"They ain't in Florida, Claude; they're in Costa Rica, don't you remember? They're on their honeymoon, Val and Jeff. And Val's the one who's wanting to stay; it's Jeff's the one who's been texting me about all the trouble. Who you think we're talking about? You gotta keep up with what's going on."

It is my firm belief that a fellow should always marry a gal who's head and shoulders smarter than he is, that way he knows he'll never be having to worry about having to worry about nothing.

We spent the rest of the evening not doing much different than usual, Donette fooling around on her phone and me scrubbing the dirt from off my shoes with a sheet of newspaper and during the news fixing myself a healthy proportion of honey buns. Ain't no way I could get her down to the beach or even go for a walk, so I just fixed us a sandwich and let the TV jaw on until it was time for going to bed. If I had any dream, it was a dream about being awake.

Next morning I put Henry into the car because I'm taking him to see the dolly museum.

"What like Dolly Parton?" says Donette, always skeptical.

"No, like GI Joe and figurines."

"What you mean like baby dolls and Hummels? Precious Moment stuff sort of thing?"

"Some of them boys on the course recommended it to us yesterday when we were out horsing around."

"I don't think Jeff will approve of you making his boy into a sissy," she goes, thumbing the screen on her phone, "but you go on and be my guest."

"He ain't no sissy so long as he stays with me."

"Just don't come back with no Barbie dolls, Claude. Jeff will not be amused."

Turns out we was both wrong. There ain't no dolls; there ain't no tribute to the lady of "My Old Tennessee Home." Turns out it's all just a bunch of junk. Strange stuff in a building made of . . . *very suggestive* glass blobs. A sort of funhouse, I suppose, for uppity smart people, and bad paintings filled with melting clocks and deserts and half-naked ladies and oddball gizmos, strange stuff made by a mad man to make a man mad. Baby Henry didn't care for it one bit. The only one I might hang up somewhere in my garage—and I'm not claiming it's even worth paying money for—I'm talking like if maybe you gave it to me as a present—was this one they had a whole chorus of angels of and in the middle of them they got this fellow pulling a boat. That I can understand. I understand you got to bring a boat ashore. That idea makes sense. Everything else was just money flushed down the commode, but I reckon I'd be more steamed up if I'd been charged a second price of admission for Baby Henry, who they let come in for free.

"Boudreaux, isn't it?" says the gal at the reception right as we're coming in. The sparkle in her eyes making me wish I was running round, forty years ahead of the wind. "I was thinking this might be of interest." She passes over a book and points with her bright red fingernail to a line there on the page.

"Am I supposed to know this?"

"That's the guest book from ninety-three. I've been typing names onto a spreadsheet all morning, and I came across this entry. I remembered you saying you used to come here way back when. Right there," she taps her nail. And sure enough unhidden there on the page is the handwriting of my wife's cursive:

Dear Allen,

Thanks for the time of a life!

xxoo

Claude and Netty Boudreaux

"Think that might be y'all two?"

"That's us all right." I hand her back the guest book. "There's sure been a lot of water drawn under the bridge since that there writing was done."

"I just thought you'd like to see."

"Yup. Thank you, doll."

Back in the condo, Donette's changed out of her pj's and done her hair and makeup and is lounging in front of the television, where she's got the volume jacked to the max. The louder it is, the more she can get all worked up about everything and the more what's happening sounds all dramatic.

"Shut the door, Claude," she says, sipping a ginger ale packed with ice cubes. "There's a hurricane coming this way, and Jeff and Valencia are fixing to come over. Everything's been evacuated. Everything's under red alert."

"Well then we gotta pack our bags and get a move on if—"

"No, a red alert in Costa Rica, Claude. Val and Jeff had to evacuate this morning, so they're flying right now to Tampa. They should be in by three o'clock."

"Why would—"

"Just hush and listen."

She's right. There's a big old storm coming their way, already hit Panama and dumped a buttload of rain on the Caribbean, and they're not sure where it'll go or how far it will move up the Gulf, but already a dozen people have drowned and it's looking like it'll hang around Costa Rica for a period of several days, which means Val and Jeff are coming, getting clear out of her way. Which is just what in fact they do. Bags and luggage and everything. Fighting with the noise over the TV, Val and Donette, as to who can make the most of it. I told Donette we ought to spring for their own room, but she insisted we'd done enough, on camping us all together, with me on the trundle and her out on the couch and all of us sharing a bathroom and only one dresser. Baby Henry was happy to see his mama, but it didn't take long for him to find himself something to cry about. Jeff has already settled himself a space on the far side of the couch.

"So how bout them Tigers?"

He's always struck me as a good kid. Like somebody with friends. He started a job earlier this year fixing up his own concession stand out there on the lake that he's hoping is going to expand. Lord, I'd tell him he's likely to go off on one thing now as another, no better than a toddler bearing off a bucket of seashells.

"You got any money on Saturday's homecoming game?"

He starts up from his phone.

"Oh you know me, Mr. Bou . . . Claude. I keep the irons in a few different fires."

"Jeff said we could go to Paris next year so long as we use half our gifts to pay down some of his credit cards," says Val.

"Claude, when we going to Paris? You know he ain't ever talked to me about taking no trip to Paris. Jeff, you coming strong out the stalls, setting the bar up mighty fast, boy."

Jeff casts up and nods and goes back to the stuff on his phone.

"Val, honey, how come—"

"Hey, what we eating for dinner?" says Val. "Ooo, I know! Let's go out for ichiban! Jeff and I lately've been getting into ichiban. We just love us some Japanese."

"Jeff, that right? You getting into Japanese?" says Donette.

"Oh, you know. It don't make no difference to me, whatever winds up in my gut."

"Somebody turn down the air," says Val.

"It is turned down. All the way to the max."

With everyone coming and going and opening all the doors, the condo is stuffy and hot.

I like to think God invented air conditions to keep women happy, but where exactly all her wants come from, where all those tastes and whims and needs, if it ain't like looking at a high-watt light bulb sometimes: you can see the brightness; you can feel the heat; but you can't look directly right at the filament . . . that is, unless, I suppose, you wear sunglasses.

Well, the next day they say twenty-four folks have perished in Costa Rica due to that storm, and now the weathermen's not sure where it could be going to next—some think round Gulf Shores, others to around New Orleans, so that the lot of us figures the best course of action is just to stay right where we're at and see what happens next. And everyone seems okay with that. Jeff has his seat staked out in the corner; Val and Donette are happy making all kinds of plans for Henry for when they get back and when he grows up that they don't mind me bumming around, watching reruns of *Moesha*. They brought back a refrigerator magnet for Donette and tried bringing me a stash of Little Debbies, but all they had over there in the grocery store, says Val, was Hostess.

"Hey, Claude, wake up!"

I must have been fast asleep.

"Wake up, Claude! You was grinding your teeth again. I'm gonna make you an appointment when we get home with Dr. Gortzman. Maybe he'll have something to say about you making them funny faces all the time."

"Papaw's been making funny faces?" says Val. Val's bouncing the baby on her knee, making funny faces at him herself. "What kind of funny faces he been doing?"

"Oh, I'm just saying sometimes he goes like *this*, and sometimes he goes like *that*! Don't you, Claude? Show them some of the funny faces you do." And the three of them have a good laugh. "He says it's only a little tic."

"Mr. Bou . . . I mean Claude, you best not keep them faces up, especially if the winds change. My grandma always said, 'You make funny faces when the wind change, your face'll like to stick that way.'"

Sure enough they're calling for that big storm to head for over the house. Both of us called out work, but it didn't matter because no one's going to work anyway if a category-two hurricane is passing right over town. The storm's a good excuse to sit by and be with family. Even if the group of us has been cooped up longer than we'd want. I do have to say it's nice just sitting around, being under one roof. Once the kids grow up, it's rare to have so much time together. Family becomes something different, feels sometimes like pretending, like a sort of make-believe of the past. But for the life of me I don't know what to do with that little message: *Thanks for the time of a life! Netty.* Ain't nobody calls her Netty no more except for me and rarely her sister, and she ain't called herself that since,

I believe, she was a twenty-four-year-old girl. It makes a man sit up and wonder, and if he ain't careful, he can allow himself to get somewhat suspicious, but I ain't never found any of that to be all that helpful. But still a man can't help but doubt. And you and all those other folks fixing to stay dead a long, long while. And then in all that thinking I can't help but also recall some things forgot in the past, stuff I forgot from so long ago. For instance, one time we had this gal, this pretty little hen of a secretary working for us with a nice set of curled-up hair. I always thought she might have been giving me the goo-goo eyes, but I didn't want to assume nothing. Then one day she up and tells me while I go running past, fanning herself:

"Mr. Claude, how come you got to be so darn handsome. You sure make it hard on a gal to get her work seen to."

"Oh, my apologies, ma'am. My apologies."

And cut my corn if some crazy ideas didn't start popping into my head that I felt like a crazy man for not acting on them, running at full speed past her desk. I believe she got married not long after that, that gal, and I don't guess I should've done different.

But that's old news and long been over.

I believe that door is closed. I believe that ship's done sailed.

The Good Life

For ten years they had been on their own, done with college and living as adults, chasing jobs with benefits and a salary and something of the good life. They had settled in many places, among them, Denver, Asheville, Nashville, Austin, Minneapolis, Portland, in apartments and neighborhoods always a little better than they could afford. There had even been three weeks in Chicago when she had worked at a Burger King while he had worked at a Waffle House.

Then it was decided. She had discerned a call to become an ordained priest, and at the same time, as if by fate, he was offered a job at the seminary working in development. So they packed up and moved to Virginia, where they adopted a little dog. Yet within three weeks he knew that he hated the work, that he hated his boss and the utter mindlessness of his colleagues, and by the middle of the fall the job proved altogether lackluster. That was when he applied for the scholarship. His proposal said he would continue with some research he had done a few years before, to some acclaim, and that spring, unexpectedly, they awarded it to him—ten months in the UK, all expenses paid, the only condition being that he write another paper. And while they would have to live apart, the timing would work out well, since during her second year it was required that she not only attend class but serve at a church and hospital. For the next year there would hardly be any time together. So he accepted the scholarship and promised to return home at Christmas.

It was by accident that he woke. Looking up, he saw a panorama of ocean and mountains: on one side of the train, the surf breaking toward the rails, on the other, bright, verdant fields rolling off toward the Highlands. Over the rocks lay a congregation of seals radiant in the sun like great things of corpulence. He remembered someone telling him why the grass was so green—something about how because of the rarity of sunlight the chlorophyll was more intense, and indeed the grass everywhere seemed almost to glow.

Within a few days he had settled into the routine he would more or less adopt for the rest of his time abroad. After mornings in the library he would go for walks on the strand or up on the bluff, trying to cast the research from his brain. He had never seen clouds moving so quickly and so close to the ground. To the north, beyond an inlet, an assembly of windmills was cutting the fog clockwise.

In the evenings there were seminars and parties to go to. Professors invited him to events that featured opulent receptions where the object of the night was to glad-hand more people than you could rightly remember the next morning. While none of the subjects much interested him, most of the people he met he treated with that easy insouciance that belongs among close friends, since he knew he would never see any of them again after ten months. But if there were times when the research felt too tedious or the people too interchangeable, he reminded himself that even the worst of it easily beat out the best of the work he had done back home.

He told his wife that all was coming along—the only problem being a mix-up with the Fife Council, which was charging him several hundred pounds in fees and utilities he had never owed and which refused to believe he had not lived in his flat when he said. He and his flatmate shared a small cottage near the end of the road by the ruins of the cathedral. His flatmate, another researcher who was visiting for the year, a pale, bald, foppish lecturer from a small school in Florida, would sometimes accompany him to one of the pubs if there were no events going on, where each listened with a show of interest to what the other had read and written that day. One night, under the influence of several rounds of bitter, they made a hearty pledge sooner to go to jail than pay the five hundred pounds in council tax.

That he talked with his wife for barely a quarter hour each day and afterward rarely thought about her seemed natural, even expected. For years he had imagined getting away (he never dwelt on leaving her, per se; however, in these imaginings they were not together, so some kind of leave-taking must have occurred, some unnoticeable, painless drifting like continental plates slowly wrenching apart), what it would be like to know other people, to live in the quiet of only his thoughts. Now there was a host of opportunities for meeting new people, for long conversations in low-lit settings, the enthusiasm of which was not so much fueled by the cider that had been imbibed or the prospect of touching bodies as by the very freedom that allowed such intimacy. He thought: Perhaps it's a sign I'm getting older, but sex in itself doesn't interest me. Far more, everything else before it.

One of these opportunities included a dinner with a woman from his department, which, having just left another event, he showed up a little drunk for. There would have been no reason from him to remember it or her had there not, a few days later, been a seminar where he ran into her and following which she invited herself along for a pint. As the night grew late, they talked less about ideas than the past. He listened and watched her eyes light up while he looked on not without a certain tenderness and, smiling, thought to himself, Yes, I know exactly how this story ends, and that's what makes it hurt, and hurt so sweetly.

At one point she sprang up from the table and began to dance (no one else in the pub was dancing) and cajoled him to come to her between the tables as you would a toddler into bad weather. But he insisted he sit in his chair.

After he walked her home, he could not stop thinking about her, making all sorts of plans, running through possible scenarios; at once he realized he had gone mad. He knew that, as with so many new acquaintances, love tended to flame out as quickly as it flared.

Within a few days they had arranged another meeting: he had suggested taking her along one of his walks up the bluff. Under her coat she had on a sleeveless houndstooth dress, and it was now that he noticed her cheeks were faintly acne scarred and that she walked with a slight dip, and though she was only twenty-four, her hair was already starting to gray, and the confidence it must have taken not to dye it served fiercely to attract him.

They went down by the ruins, then by the harbor and onto the strand, which led toward the bluff, all the while taking care to share the path while not brushing hands. Twice a day the sea incarnated the rocks with a quilt of seaweed: when it came, everyone could smell the muck all over town. A luminous fog lay in the distance, though the weather remained wholly blustery. Dark bodies dotted the beach, which, seeming to hold their place, gave the late morning a staged sort of randomness. She had one leg that was shorter than the other and told him about the many operations she had undergone—eighteen—and she admitted that the first time she had ever lied was at the age of four, to her parents about not being in pain. (Later that night, as he was falling asleep, he supposed she had told many people the same stories in an effort to win their sympathies, but that they may have been rehearsed did not diminish their beauty.) He told her his wife was currently working at a hospital.

"Which one?"

He told her the name of the hospital.

"I spent some time at that hospital. What wing of it is she at?"

"I don't know. You were there for an operation?"

"No. I had a friend who was there for two weeks in the psych ward after she tried to kill herself. I visited her every day. I was also there when I overdosed on acetaminophen."

They were going up the bluff. Through yarrow, patches of knapweed, lady's bedstraw, saxifrage. Below them the sand was slithering toward the surf like the smoke of fires just extinguished.

"You tried to commit suicide?"

"There's a distinction to be made between actively trying to kill yourself and wanting to. I wouldn't have spent only a night in the ER if I hadn't told them I'd taken too much by accident."

"Was that because of a breakup?"

"Yes. Because of a breakup."

They were almost at the top of the bluff. The brush hung under the weight of dew or the night's rain. He admired the drops in their chance perfection. Peering in, he tilted one of the dozens of white trumpet-shaped flowers that were in bloom alongside the path: inside its cradle lay a fat bee asleep, the rump of him jutting out.

They stood there for a time, at the top of the bluff. The town looked small and closer together than it was. Below, seagulls gathered from the rocks and moved toward the opposite end of the strand, drifting loosely like bits of paper.

Wondering whether he should forge ahead, he said:

"You have an appreciation for life that is remarkable despite such suffering in your past."

He glanced in her direction. There was no reply. At the corners of her eyes tears were brimming, and she moved on suddenly, leading with that slight dip.

Far down the bluff, like a castle from a fairy tale, and behind a shimmering haar like a painted background from an old movie set that lends the verisimilitude of depth, was the Fairmont, which they agreed was their destination. An hour later they reached it drenched (it had rained, been sunny, and then rained again) and more worn out than they were expecting, and they ordered cheap champagne that instantly went to their heads. Within minutes she had sprung up and was dancing. Her tiny body swaying and dipping, enlivened as though with stuff from the origin of time. He settled back contentedly into his chair. It was a bar of some refinement; everyone in the room in their gowns and dinner jackets was watching her, sizing up that incredible motion. He wished she would go on dancing that way forever.

"Your partner . . . Astrid, does she—"

"*They.*"

"Do they like to dance?"

"Come here."

He downed the rest of the glass of champagne with the commitment of making an ass of himself.

As he was kissing her later that night, he thought: I am a man who cheats on his wife.

As the days began to shorten, they continued seeing each other. The days she did not come by, he felt, were merely stepping stones to get to the days she did. Some nights when he had failed to see her, he wondered whether she was out dancing or could be bringing some other man to her bed, and often on such reflections he caught and told himself that none of it really mattered and was surprised by how quickly he made himself not care. Indeed, he smiled at himself whenever he observed the onset of jealousy, doubt, the urge for possession, giddiness, anticipation, feelings that he had long not associated with any particular woman. He liked seizing the small content of her body and letting go the kisses that had been waiting to scamper off his lips. Now and then she complained that his beard gave the skin around her mouth a rash, yet in a way that conveyed he should go on doing it. The nights they stayed over, before they went to bed, she would record long messages to her partner in Spanish. He was never sure of a word of whatever she said, but something about the whole ordeal gave him comfort. Ere the terns flew he kept waiting for the falling out.

"He just goes on and on forever. Once I clocked him at forty-five minutes. He talks himself into whatever he believes of the second, convincing himself as he says it, divagates, then ends up in total contradiction, and then contradicts himself again. My primary relevance in life was being an echo to the sounding board of the universe's void. It just served to show that most people's ideas are castles built on quicksand, and ones that crumble at the slightest wind. But you can't take shelter in sand castles. And you can't outrun your shadow. Rog reminds me of him very vaguely."

"Mine was the same way. I remember in court they asked me if I could ever forgive him. I said, 'Yes. I'd be willing to forgive him if he writes me a letter in which he admits to everything and everyone he's wronged.' That's all he had to do. And sign his name."

"Did he?"

"Of course not. I knew he was too solipsistic to do anything of the sort. After that I never saw him again."

Of all that accounted for their quick leap to intimacy, he was grateful that his flesh proved a constant source of delight for her—and this no novice's delight of discovery (from what he gleaned, she had known many lovers) but one by which him feeling pleasure gave her pleasure as well. He felt like a worn-out dog in the lap of its sensitive master who knows precisely where and how to scratch it, a creature with no concept of pleasure and pain, something that is merely made to feel. For so long he had abandoned the body in favor of the head. But what is the head without the body? The answer, of course, is nothing. As the peak of her pleasure was approaching, she would start whispering a soft Spanish. He had to look up what *cielo* and *cariño* meant.

He was keeping to his routine of studying in the morning and then going for walks in the afternoon before returning to the library, the intrusions of her name, of something she had said, of a memory from their time together forming the primary object of his attention, with everything else relegated to a sort of background mechanics. Rarely did she ask about his wife and rarely did he mention her, for, as a rule, he tried to refrain from talking about the problems they had been having, since he felt such talk would be an unjust plea for sympathy. But as the winter break drew near, she was accounted more and more space in their conversations so that she became almost a living presence with them in the room.

"Talk to your wife," she told him.

"We do talk, every day."

"About what's bothering you."

"It's not so simple." Then as an afterthought: "You'll see. Once you and Astrid have been together ten years, you'll come to accept your fate with a certain amount of . . . *happy resignation.*" She gave him one of those looks that said he should probably stop talking.

"So you don't feel guilty?"

The question caught him off guard. For a while he had wondered whether it was something she wondered about, until he had quit wondering about it himself. While she continued to pack, he sat on the bed, thinking—or rather, waiting for any thought. Finally he told her, "There are times I do and times I don't. Perhaps one day I will ask her for forgiveness when I can be sure she will forgive me."

His wife was still very busy over the winter break in the strain and stress of her own device, and much of the time it was just he and the dog settled beside each other in the living room or walking around the seminary. Often he ran into colleagues and acquaintances from the previous year. He kept waiting for a message, but some kind of unspoken game of chicken was being played between them as to who would be the first to write—he was sure she must have been thinking about him as he was thinking about her; he had written three versions of a message, each at varying levels of passion. In the meantime, holiday plans, preparations, and purchases each came embodying a new string of impossible fantasies. When Christmas Eve arrived, she was finally reprieved from work, and they packed up the car and drove the ten hours to his parents. For the whole trip they hardly shared a word, and the view of the gray land beyond the windows seemed almost nonexistent, a place at the end of creation whose only value was as a canvas over which to imagine Catalina.

All during Christmas Day—through the presents, the welcoming of friends and relatives, the preparation and enjoying of dinner—she was his whole mind. Each event invoked a profound new meditative grief. He thought: This woman will never see inside my old closet; she will never taste the milk punch my father makes; she will never be anywhere near me on Christmas morning. And when suddenly the revelation that the day was almost over for her (she was seven hours ahead!) dawned on him with the brutality of the moment, his utter thoughtlessness compelled him to send her the most passionate message he had been saving. To have not sent any greeting whatsoever on Christmas seemed one of the worst acts of cruelty he could inflict. Within ten minutes he received a response—far longer than the one he had sent, but hers filled with details of the day and her own celebrations, which incited him to wonder whether she were an extremely rapid typer or whether she had composed hers earlier and had simply been waiting for his in order to send hers. He spent the rest of that evening reading his message then hers, as though it comprised an actual dialogue, and he could now say to himself that the day had not been wasted.

When they got back to the seminary, there were a few weeks before she resumed her work and before he recrossed the Atlantic. At nights the two of them drank some of the wine they had been saving and watched movies they had talked about wanting to see, or perhaps someone would come over and entertain them, and there were moments when he could almost convince himself he was happy, that the future, as it looked, looked hospitable and without grief. Yet no matter his contentment, he could not help always comparing them. He missed kissing the scars on her leg. He felt his wife was not adequately comprehending life's pleasure. (For instance, one evening, as they were cooking, a song came on and he began to dance as he had those times with Catalina, coaxing his wife into joining him in the kitchen, but she looked at him like he was crazy.) For her, making love seemed less a sort of surrendering and more a compulsory duty, a type of mandatory resignation. Moreover, he would be in the midst of talking to her, his wife, and would notice something, perhaps her hair or the way she did her eyebrows, perhaps the phrasing of what she had said, and would weigh her along these lines against Catalina, as if in the balance of fate: Her hair, it looks like Catalina's; or, Catalina's eyebrows are slightly more angled and go further down in front of the eyes, are thinner; or Catalina's arguments and observations are much more substantial, but less wholesome, and yet oddly far more refined. At one point she had even mentioned something along the lines of the possibility of an open relationship, of trying out a marriage that might navigate a few affairs, but he could not bring himself to pursue the subject further: something about her even having to say such a thing struck him as profoundly sad.

At the airport they said goodbye, kissing with a fair amount of passion wherein it was hard to tell what was real and what was feigned.

"Come back to me," she told him.

From the day he had arrived back in the States he had been looking forward to returning to his life without consequence, but on walking into his apartment, he scented that he and his flatmate had had a falling out. Was it a falling out if he was unaware of what had happened? Somebody else had to fill in the gaps since Rog would no longer speak to him. Come to find out, Rog had been arrested. Having returned a few days ahead of the term, his flatmate had settled back into the routine of research when the Fife Council came knocking on the door with a warrant for both their arrests, but since Rog was the only one present, there had been a night spent in jail alone, with the parents not only having to pay the bail and the processing fees but the initial five hundred pounds they had so flagrantly scorned to fork over. In fact, Rog's family was so upset that if he refused to pay half of all the expenses, they were threatening to sue.

Which was to say he had been looking forward to escaping to the holy space of her bed, yet as a result of a slight lag in her correspondence (he found out later it was because of a trip to the hospital), which in consequence caused him to delay his, what was supposed to be their grand reunion ended up a vague calling to accounts. At any rate, it was around this time that he was able finally to put a finger on her primary fault: apart from a few eccentricities like she could not stand to touch a bare foot on the floor and got violently ill on trains, she could not bear to be alone. Always she was running into somebody or making new friends or plans for parties or coffee, was always cutting short their rendezvous for some new date; she could never be by herself. And it was this essential fault that worked to diminish her in his esteem, as if her company might stand to be more selective. Then after a while he thought, It doesn't matter. If it wasn't this, it would be something else.

Having been intimate for several months, he could now confide that so much of his initial attraction had been merely the need to be physical, to be desired and touched, a need that he had disguised from himself as a kind of chancing of kindred hearts. Yet rather than viewing this with cynicism or outright dismissiveness, as an incentive for pulling away, he was glad the way things had turned out. He thought: If we were still mad about each other, would it be possible I would know her as well as I do?

As the nights began to shrink and their slipping hold on the daylight seemed to presage some defect in the fabric of time and delight, as winter parkas one by one returned to their summer hiding places, they were making plans for her to host her partner for the week. He offered to disappear until the moment her partner was gone. But she insisted her partner was fine with the whole affair, with everything, in fact had encouraged her to become more intimate, and merely wanted to meet, having heard so much about everything. That week he kept trying to alight on a good reason that would compel him to be out of town, some dire visit across the country he owed somebody or to some remote library for some random footnote necessary for his paper, while at the same time he kept waiting for her call: he kept wondering whether she would invite him to stay the night or join them on a date as a prelude to getting him in the sack with the both of them—but she never did—and the dinner she planned ended up turning out rather pleasant.

"Thank you for arranging a lovely dinner," he was telling her the next day. "I hope Astrid had a good stay."

"Yes. Astrid thought you were very charming, which doubtless you always are. They're excited about incorporating your thoughts on residual orality into their thesis. They're hoping to get you to Oxford . . . that is, if I allow it."

For the whole evening their stomachs had been making uncomfortable noises. Even after all this time they had never come to a working solution for the issue of noisy bowels.

"That would be wonderful. She really has a first-rate mind. I wish—"

"*They* have a first-rate mind, which by the way sounds utterly naff and condescending."

"*They*, yes, *they*: I'm so sorry. *They*, yes, unlike me: who has a very fourth-rate mind. I keep running up against my stupidity."

Twice she had told him "I love you." Once, when they were returning home from dancing at an upscale bar, she had pulled him aside from the streetlamps, into an unlit door, and, after kissing him fervently around the ear, whispered, "I love you so much," but he had chosen not to utter the words back. At the time he told himself he had not said them because they were both a little drunk, and he was uncertain how much she had really meant them—if she had just been too afraid to have told him in the past or if it were merely the inebriation that had spurred her too far forward. Then a few months later she had written in a message: ". . . and of course I love you very dearly." And again it was a predicament. Of course he loved her the same. But then he could rightly affirm that he loved everybody on some level; everybody was worthy of love; he had no problem telling any stranger he met on the street that truly he loved them, loved all humanity. Still, he did not want his first time saying it not to be in person, so he decided to hold off for a better occasion. Later he wondered whether it was this slight pulling back that had made her in turn not seek him out for the next several days.

While there were still several months until she would graduate, with the end in mind they made plans to get away to the mountains—to a cabin with a hot tub—where the goal was to lounge around naked for the weekend and drink champagne, a kind of last hurrah before the inevitable pulling away that would accompany the onset of summer. At their cabin, which looked nothing like the pictures and where the hot tub had become a grave for snails and deliquescing leaves and where the mountains remained bearded in fog, they lived under the sheets, only rarely venturing out as if into a hazardous element. For barely an hour each day there was no rain, though it scarcely mattered. He chanced on new particulars of her body he had not happened on before, moles whose coordinates he should have been able to locate by now, scars whose mysterious hieroglyphs signified a buried prehistory as yet unknown. There they finally made love. By this point he was well aware that it would be unremarkable, that he would look back and see so little that was inspired among that tackle of skin, only another occasion for the passing tide of guilt. But something about its purity worked to arrest him, and afterward he held on to her for a long time as though she were some kind of last hope for salvation. By the end of the trip her entire face glowed from being kissed. The days were so long now that light itself seemed inherent to darkness.

Not long after they got back his wife informed him that she was coming to stay for the summer (after some problems obtaining a visa, she had worked it out with the seminary that she could take classes abroad) and had found a classmate to watch the dog. However, before he had time to process it all, she and her partner were suddenly broken up. The rupture had made sense; they were wanting to go their separate ways, and Astrid had met somebody in Oxford. There were no real hard feelings.

"We're still good friends. In fact, we talked this morning about their article on Homeric epithets in eighteenth-century protest literature. They're really quite happy. We just realized some things would never change."

"I never committed to marriage expecting to change anything," he offered hastily, as if in covering something up. "I just thought I'd get more used to their problems is all."

"Like how you got used to mine?"

He sighed. He had been through this on every angle.

"We'd get tired of each other or fight about something stupid. That's the way it always ends."

"Not if you end it first," she said, and when he kept looking at her: "Ends are also beginnings."

During those last weeks before his wife was set to arrive, he continued his routine of research in the morning (the paper was nearly finished, and he had the summer to explore the country before returning home to the seminary) and going on long walks on the strand or the bluff, now and then seeing Catalina. He was drinking less those weeks, intent on meeting the evening in a state in which he would make himself feel the strain of being alone. Once he gazed down on the beach and chanced upon a still-limp starfish. He thought: None of it really matters anyway. But this is better than some things.

Every day he was deliberating whether or not to marry her, tabulating the pros and cons in the hope that the balance would clearly favor a certain outcome. So often when they were together, he felt like he was standing outside himself, castigating himself for not appreciating her, for taking for granted these final sad moments. There was briefly talk of incorporating his wife into the affair, but the idea soon dissipated to another false start.

The night before his wife was set to arrive, they went to the most expensive restaurant in town and sat across from each other in silence. Speaking felt wholly useless; any verbalization felt preordained. At one point in the meal she rose effortlessly from her chair and started swaying in rhythm to the piano. He stood and drew her near, and they danced like that between the tables of diners like people in some private world.

"I know, I know."

"Shut up," she told him. "Quit faffing around and remember."

As she lay beside him a final time, he sat there thinking about whether or not to marry her.

Well, I'm one kind of coward or another, he thought.

He was back at his place by the cathedral. They had said their goodbyes an hour ago, and he had just stepped out of the shower. Still wet, he had lathered his cheeks and chin, the straight razor reared to his neck. His wife had messaged him that her train had left the station, and there were less than thirty minutes until he was picking her up from the bus.

Now, as he looked at himself in the mirror, what looked back was unsettling, a person he was supposed to know but whose features seemed somehow removed. The gray in the hair, the lines at the dark sides of the eyes, the random mottling of hickeys or spots along the shoulders, the general weariness of the stare—it looked at him more like out of a photograph than someone he was attached to. Not only the figure itself but the eyes he saw the scene through: it felt the same way after he had run or was jet-lagged or had been reading far too long. Like watching someone he cared about, but only up to a certain point. His sight had become beguiled by too much beauty.

He thought: I can do anything right now and say I had a good life.

The Summer We Ate Off the China

SHE HAS BEEN KNEELING over the toilet, arms on the cool of the seat, when the light goes off on the phone. From the far side of the bed the man turns from watching her and reads the number without any name and is about to ask, "Shall I answer it?" but before he is able, he hears it coming up into the bowl.

When at last she turns off the light and goes to the bed, so long has it been she would have thought he were sound asleep, but she finds him awake, waiting there, knows he has deliberately stayed awake and is waiting to speak as he coaxes her to his arms.

After a while he clears his throat.

"Everything all right?"

"Yes."

"Are you sure?"

"It's only a headache."

Her answer seems to satisfy him, and they lie there on the bed unmoving except for the shallow breathing until eventually he squeezes her tightly while he whispers to the back of her head.

"I love you so much. I always will."

An hour until the event.

She is standing over the tables, where she sorts and sets the silverware, folds the napkins into tiers of equal threes, arranges the glasses so that the spine of the knife is tangent to the outside of the water glass while looking for smudges that are then cleared on the hem of the apron, going along the pulled-back jacquard drapery and cherry wainscoting and the portraits of long-dead dons and clergy whose faces of dour wrinkles give the impression they have done nothing but be extinct, preserve the indefinite death of forebears, now and then returning to the kitchen to refill the tray or replace a glass with another that is unstreaked by suds from the wash, the mounting ache in the feet, even after standing night after night in the uniform black slippers that are well broken in, sometimes overcoming these efforts to beat the clock so that there almost arises the need to sit, and indeed once the guests start to arrive, she is standing over the tables still, adjusting linens, adding, removing chairs, setting and lighting candles, filling glasses from a pewter pitcher (the pitcher is wrapped with linen to soak the condensation that might fall on the laps of guests) that is repeatedly returned to the kitchen to be refilled, putting down bread still warm with toasting, their tops having been brushed with egg white and sprinkled with Cornish salt, cleaning up spills, answering requests and inquiries, even suffering herself to be accosted by a gentleman with a club pin on his lapel who casually slips a gratuity into the apron in return for the act of setting it there, the hand feigning at not making contact with this woman on the careful face of whom there are no freckles but a dark mole above the upper lip and another before the temple that is half hidden by the tied-back hair, the noise in the hall steadily climbing to a roar, a sea whose turbulent surge is a constant clinking of silverware and donors shouting over each other to be heard, so loud and riotous, unavoidable, she knows merely by the nod of his head that it is time to clear the hors d'oeuvres, that he will call her later . . . later . . .

At her apartment, the lights turned off, shoes cast off on the floor not far behind her, she stares at the light shining under the door, waits for his knock. In the Underground the headache returned, and though there were few people out at the hour, she would not let herself do anything but wait for the train to come barreling down through its wormhole, that and check the phone.

He said he was stopping by after work. He said he had never had feelings for anyone before like the feelings he felt for her and he hoped she understood.

Now she waits for the shadow, for the light to be interrupted in the hall, for the knock to come at the door, and while she waits she listens to the message from the number she does not know.

"Hello, Maggie. It's Lisa Erskine. I hope you don't mind . . . it's a bit bad. I don't suppose you remember; ever since the accident Morris's required a bit of some extra care—yes, now that I'm having a think on it, I suppose it's all news to you. But the thing of it is I'm in a bit of a kinch with my ticker. They're saying I don't have very much longer, only maybe another month or so. So we were thinking—honestly hoping—if you'd be for coming to Muckross, if there's anything of Collum's you care to take home, something, some kind of memento, you'd be more than welcome to come have a look. Take what you want. Only, being you studied law, I'd be quite grateful for any suggestion so they don't go taking the house. You can reach us at East Neuk Care on Market . . ."

Even after the message has ended and she is listening to air, or attuned to the sound of the voice in her memory, and even then not so much remembering, hearing the bumbling weight of the voice and knowing what is meant by what has been said, as feeling the nonplus of darkness and silence required to anchor these words to some authentic potential of being and resolution, to dissolve them and forget, it is only the knock at the door, the light abrupted by shadow that recalls her to where she is—the night, the floor, a headache—that reminds her she is waiting for the shadow to go away.

For the last four hours she has been hunched on the seat of the train, holding and squeezing her knees, head against the cool of the window and eyes pinched hard to stop out the light overhead in the car and the lowering sun as they wind farther along up the sea, and still is, curled on herself, the day having almost turned to dusk, and they have passed York now, have passed that stout cathedral established by the victorious Normans that holds the incorruptible relics of the reluctant and holy saint, the bridges of industrial Newcastle keeping their ironwork vigil over the slumbering Tyne, when the conductor, with a light tap to the shoulder, offers some paracetamol, thinking she has taken too much to drink, which she forgoes with a wave of the hand.

The cab that took her to the inn drove for barely a minute—she had remembered the size of the village but not the proximity of the station—though she would not have walked had she recalled this still. Too dark to see anything except cobblestones and fronts of lime harling made anonymous by the harsh light of the lamps. The braking and turns bearing the outline of familiarity. At the inn she goes to the pub and orders a room.

"Business or pleasure?"

"Neither," she says, taking the key.

"Come only to get away?"

She goes to the room and, without switching on the light, lies down on the bed. She does not take off shoes and socks, nor does she stretch out and grab the pillow and think how luxurious it feels to stretch out on a big bed in a new country, nor does she note the faint odor of gorse on the thick white sheets. There is a TV, a view of the harbor, a phone, and a painting in acrylic of a bird. The throbbing in her temples, when it ebbs, leaves little room in its wake but dread of the next wave.

After a while she picks up the phone and sends the message she has been planning:

Sorry, not feeling well. X

A few moments later the light goes off and she reads the following, which she has expected more or less to read:

Came by last night but you weren't there? Yes of course.
Shall I stop by after work? You're amazing! X

She stares at the phosphorous glow of the screen until it goes off. She has read the words and memorized them, and now she repeats them, waits for their meaning to subside until they are no longer signifiers that bear relation to time or history, sets down the phone by the bed, and takes up the key.

"What's this?"

"Aye, 'warm pudding'? Don't the Swiss prefer you to read?"

"It's not my reading, Don, needs mending; it's these dodgy descriptions that account for the lack of a proper menu. 'Fish and chips,' okay. 'Hamburger,' I don't take any real issue. 'Bangers and mash,' all right, well done. But 'warm pudding' I draw the line. That could mean almost about anything. Sticky toffee, melted ice cream, warm chocolate cake, or candy bar you set in the microwave."

"It's actually—"

"No, Don, your descriptions are wasted on the likes of an unimaginative mind such as myself. If I cared about what I was eating, I'd've gone down the street to the bistro, wouldn't I?"

"To Plat du Prince?" says the other man beside him, his friend.

"That's it precisely. Instead of 'warm pudding,' you'd find something there along the lines of *'le dessert chaud,'* which, simply for the sake of being in French, already renders the same ambiguous item a hundred times more delectable, and under the heading of which, I'm sure, is a sumptuous meditation, a feast for the general eyes, something along the lines of: *le dessert chaud* is composed of grain culled from the courageous plains of Culloden, where it has been combed daily by the Highland winds and matured under the gaze of a fickle Caledonian sun, just as the milk, which we here extol under the name of 'sweet cream,' was derived from the udders of indomitable beeves who grazed on the graves of Glencoe and coerced by the milk-white fingers of virtuous Jacobite maidens who, drawing forth this milk brose by which in reading you are truly about to taste, sang forty-two 'Charlie My Darlings' while the sparrows of the field accompanied her in melodious counterpoint and the swank and steeve fillies raised up their tongues in merry neighs. The raisins, equal no less to the finest of Burgundy, dried in the tropic sun—"

"I'll order that, please," says the friend.

"Sorry," says the bartender, reclaiming the chalkboard, "all we got's warm pudding. Hiya, would you like any drink for you?" he asks the woman who has come to the bar.

"May I recommend the warm pudding," says Andy, after the bartender has finished her order. "Here on business?" In response to which she shrugs. "Cold as the North Sea are we? Oh, right, 'neither business nor pleasure.' A little bird told me. And judging by the likes of you, I'd say you were the friendliest ever to come north."

The other man sitting at the bar says something, and the two of them confer.

"Will you let us buy you a drink?" says Andy.

"No, thank you," says the woman.

"A wee hair of the dog? Or perhaps a tactical chunder is more in order?"

"It's not like that," she says.

"Teetotaler are we?"

"No."

"Right. I've played all my cards."

The other, approaching after some hesitation, says, "I'm Alasdair, and let me offer you my apologies on behalf of the voice of my friend. The two of us were friends—"

"Key word being *were*."

"—ever since we were lads, and he's always been off his trolley. Without any harm. He's manager with Forbo Nairn, and I'm in Leven right now on business, leading a training for the coastguard. It's a beautiful village, aside from being a two-pub town."

"I believe our slogan should be: Muckross, a place you didn't know you didn't want to be. A beggar's mantle fringed with coal."

"Aye, there's another lovely description."

"That's Jimmy the Sixth, whose words have well stood the endurable test of time. Four centuries no less. Take my dad as an illustration: spent every day working by the light of fish heads in the mines of Kirkcaldy. Owned barely a thread in his sweater. And thousands of folks just like him. Your dad as well."

"Aye."

"You're lucky for your education. He went down to London—to your neck of the country—and now he's paid for saving lives. Search and rescue teams he calls it."

"Did you hear all the helicopters flying overhead this morning—that's us, I'm afraid."

"I only arrived," she says.

"Oh, right. Well, you will then tomorrow. And I offer my pre-emptive apologies."

"Here's hoping you have a restful night's sleep."

"Fish supper." The bartender sets down her plate.

"Might I bring this upstairs?"

"The plate, you mean, to your room? That's fine. But don't walk away with my plate. I'd only feel comfortable making these gents eat off the wood."

"So long," they say, but she has already left to eat on the bed upstairs.

She woke to ghosts of a dream unlived.

It was early, and she lay in the bed very still except for the shallow breathing as the light around the curtains grew stronger, the barking of the seagulls perched on the chimneys redounding off the stone, slate, and moss, heard down by the harbor. Already the lobstermen have returned from their run, and a man in waders is pressure-washing the brine from the creels while a gaggle of sailors are sipping coffee and confer on a boat, a seagull watching them from the hawsers with the hauteur of its snide yellow eye. The tide is going out, and in the revelation of mud a heron stalks, darts his strong orange bill in a pool and lifts up proudly his catch, which is flexing in the dawn. Not far behind them, in an open atelier within what appears to be a warehouse-converted-to-garage, two men in jumpsuits repair the creels. As the one, with flourishes of sparks, welds the old gleed, the other is hunched at his needle and twine. To study the exercise of his hands, the rhythmic threading and pull, one might guess he were at some endless cat's cradle, were knitting some entanglement to ensnare all the world's felons, but not before long he pauses, halts at his loom, draping this twine-become-warp over a pot new restored, upon which instant he takes up his needle and thread and resumes his motions of earlier. And now a formation of red and white helicopters charges the harbor, where, on reaching the surf, the pairs of them divide, one side toward the bluff, the other out toward the bay, the drone having grown to a deafening roar that, even when they are out of sight, lingers in the ears, a vespine hum.

Soon children, besuited in navy blue blazers lined with gilded thread, scatter over the sidewalks, their hair yet lank from their baths not an hour ago, the gowl renewed around their eyes, shouting and gesticulate as they struggle to keep up with friends, the smell of young leaves in the rising spring sun flooding both parts of town, overpowering the aroma of the strand laid bare of the tide, the vines encroaching between the crinks in the coping of the old village walls among which magpies are already driving off pigeons to the cobblestones to waddle and search for crumbs, above them the seagulls in flight blown back on the updrafts, the offing in their eyes as they regress ever farther inland, higher.

They will arrive where they need.

"Are you kin?"
"No."
"Then you must be a friend?"
"Not really."
"Then a friend of a friend?"
"No, not exactly."
"Just a stranger you are passing through?"
"I'm an old acquaintance."
"Right, it'll be a minute if you'd care to have a seat."

She has been sitting in the bed, she and the man at her side, watching the television—they are not so much following the program as they are waiting for her reaction, perhaps to a commercial that will come on about medicine or Lotto, or perhaps to the too-gaudy dress worn by the soap-opera femme fatale, or perhaps the reaction will occur more as a recollection, as a memory or direction regarding some chore to be done, to the man who sits in the chair by the bed and who works at his hands, though he is not working, only sitting.

"A visitor," says the nurse, who introduces the woman and goes.

"Maggie! Oh thank heavens, you came! What a glorious, great surprise! Morris, it's Maggie. You remember, Collum's fiancée from donkey's years. Come over and pull up a chair."

The man—it is unclear whether or not he knows her: he has looked up once and smiled, a courteous nod above the fiddling of hands, but such a gesture may be mere politeness since he makes no follow-up display of familiarity or allusion that he recalls her from fifteen years back.

"Come up for the day?"

"I came up last night."

"And you're staying in town?"

"The Golf Inn."

"That's Greg Wishart's boy running it now, I believe. Lovely little place. But it must've been three or four years since I last set foot inside. Please, do come over and take up a chair. You're not running off? Lord knows Morris and I will take all the help we can get these days."

"I can't stay," she says, touching but not sitting down in the chair. "I have a job."

"I understand," says the woman. "Kids these days, they're so used to running around, going every which way and corner, can't sit still for a second and smell the breeze. In my day even going to town was considered a great event. When Collum said he was off for London, I knew right then there'd be no tying that boy down. He'd been running off to Dundee for painting every chance he could slip away. What kind of law is it you're practicing these days? Please say 'estate.' Oh please say 'estate law' for the love of Jesus you're practicing. Morris and me'll take all the help we can get sorting this business of wills."

"I'm not practicing. If it's any help, Scottish law can be quite different, so I'd like as not be lost on setting out."

The old man continues twisting and pulling some imaginary string, smiling toward the point in the bed where the woman's feet protrude in the covers, smiling at nothing. Or perhaps he is smiling at everything.

"But surely you have some friends, some friend of a friend who can help guide us along, guide us in the right direction with sorting this business of debt management plans, so they don't come pulling the house right out from under Morris's feet. I just want him to have a roof over his head, you know—that and a warm meal is all. Florian and the lads have promised to help with meals. Surely you must have a friend."

"I'll try to think."

"Well think hard, deary, and quick. They say I'm lucky if I can string myself along for another full month. I'll be lucky to see the rapeseed. Morris'll never forgive me if they turn him out of the house. If I'd known I'd sunk all my savings in mischance on the Lena, I'd just as soon let her sink. A feast for the barnacles and things at the bottom of the world. I tell you, growing up, you make so many mistakes—it's becoming a sorrier version of yourself. If I'd had the foresight how much all the repairs were for the costing, I'd just as soon let her sink—just as if I'd known about there'd been that storm, I'd never have let Collum go that day from the house. I'm sometimes sure she passed a minister or been built in an eclipse. It's a sorrier sort of yourself, growing up: just look at these tubes and tanks. I prove my point. But you go by the house and have you a poke around. If there's anything of Collum's you care to take, anything you see fit to want, you claim it as good as yours. You'll do that, Maggie?"

"There's really nothing I need."

"Wait," she grabs the man's wrist, which twists under her grasp. "The china. I was having a think on it only this morning. There's china up under the bed. Me and Morris never used it save only the once, but for the summer once we were married—a wedding gift it was from Morris's Great-Aunt Frey. We were saving it until we could come up in the world, you know, but all it did was serve dust. You take it, every piece of it with you home. Morris knows but eating off paper plates, and they'll auction it off with the rest of the portables, so you go and grab what you want before it falls prey to strangers and bankers. The door's wide open. It's up there under the bed. And while you're sorting through everything, you have yourself a good think on this business of the estate. You think of some way there is to save us. You'll do that, won't you, Maggie?"

She has been sitting on the carpet, between the bed and a worn side table whose support is a ship wheel on which a lamp, some crumpled magazines, and a partly drunk bottle of Irn-Bru reside—sitting and scarcely thinking. She has come into the house, into the cramped, low hall, passing the warmth of the oil-burning cooker in the kitchen, and gone up the stairs and passed without looking at the pictures hung on the walls, passed without looking at the shut door to the bedroom she once spent hours in—she can still remember the water stain on the ceiling in the shape of Belarus, the Dürer prints over the desk, the Munich self-portrait, the view of the signs on the street—and gone straight to the room where the china is.

In the yard, among the periodic barking of seagulls, a few of them stamp their feet, mimicking the effect on the lawn of rain, now and then pausing to see whether worms have come up at the feint.

At last she pulls out from under the bed a large plastic container and removes the lid. Inside are stacks of cups, saucers, and flatware protected in bubble wrap. She picks up a creamer, undoes the tape, unwinds the wrap. The creamer is in pristine condition. A gold trim runs along the handle, base, and aperture, and within the bone-white luster she can make out the reflection of the sun coming off the mirror up behind her. She imagines using the pitcher for a tea, the cups and saucers, the sugar bowl; there will be a delightful spread of biscuits, fruits, and sandwiches, a nondescript music playing smartly in the background, a fire in the fireplace, and a table set with linen, and before she can imagine who is thanking her for hosting such a nice tea, she has returned the piece to its wrapper, snapped on the lid of the tub, and slid the container back under the bed.

A number she does not recognize. Somewhere in London. A friend?

"Hello?"

"Margaret. I'm sorry for calling like this, on the phone of a friend. The trouble is I dropped mine and am presently in desperate want of a replacement. I hope you don't think I'm too crafty?"

"It's fine. What is it?"

"Is everything all right?"

"Yes, of course."

"So then you'll be at work?"

She sighs, lies down on the bed, rubbing her temple. "I'm still laid under with a migraine. But I intend on returning soon. Will that do?"

"Yes, of course. Shall I come by tonight after work? I could make myself very useful as a nurse."

In the pause she does not so much gather her thoughts as brace herself to say what she must.

"Edward, I don't think this is going to work."

Beyond the window she can hear men shouting down at the harbor. A gull.

"What? Why not?"

"Because . . . you make me feel more alone."

"But I said 'I love you.'"

"Yeah," she says, "I know."

When she goes downstairs to order the meal that she will bring back to eat on the bed, she is startled to find in the parlor a loud band of three men playing music and another man calling out steps to those—aside from the ones who are pushed to the walls and drinking on the crammed-in chairs—lining up, closing in, pairing up, swinging round, breaking up, and lining again together, only to repeat the steps with a new partner, and then again, again.

Once the music stops, she orders the meal.

"Hello."

A male voice behind her.

"Right." It is the man from last night, not the talkative one. "Would you care to dance?"

"Sorry."

"See, I was hoping you'd say yes."

"I've a bit of a headache, I'm afraid."

"Well, seeing as dancing is the body's forgiveness to itself, I'm thinking I may hold the cure."

After she turns back toward the bar, she feels a slight tap come testing the stuff in her shoulder.

"If you dance with me only this once, I promise never to ask you for anything ever again."

The music resumes, the fiddle filling the room with its dizzying promise of order over which the barker explains the sequence of steps, and now on they go, forward, around, whirling and clasping hands, sundering only to meet in another part of the parlor, opposite where they were, whirling in a rushing, roaring whirlpool set about as much by the music as passion, swirling in pairs in what seems a riptide of chaos within a maelstrom of riptides each, the laughter part of the music as she cries out not to be spun but a turn, in spite of which he spins her hopelessly out of it all so that they are struggling to keep back up, the whirling, rushing confusion, and on they go and on . . .

She wakes to the call of a seagull, the pale dark fringing the blinds and imbuing the room with a suggestion of space, the weight of the slept-in clothes still on her and the arm of the man draped over her chest.

Carefully she slides from the bed, taking the key, and then slowly, soundlessly turning the door. Outside all is quiet. At this hour there is no car on the road, no pedestrian on the sidewalk— only the pad of her steps and the rote of the far-off surf. She realizes she is going down to the harbor, where already she can smell the scent of the creels, which, together with the tide, smell something like a wet dog, and in the faint portent of the day she can see there is no one about on the beach, the low tide meaning the boats will not be back for several hours, and it is not until her flight has reached the bluff and climbed high above the town and sea and fulmars that now and then leave and return on flapless wings, the broad sky freaked with the beginning of pink, that she realizes why she has come. Wishes she had not.

His hands. Their imprint shaped in prayer. A soft tracery of veins, azure. She feels them against her scalp, how he laughed at her purring and looked on with green and sensitive eyes. The aroma of gorse is as strong as the memory itself. She is lying on his bed.

"He didn't turn back."

She has curled up on the path and is holding herself.

"Oh come back. Come back please, for anything."

He has been standing before his workbench, undergoing the gestures accompanied by needle and twine, pulling and twisting the thread that he fashions into his unfinished warp of loops, the voices of children on their way to school hushed when the bands of them stop and watch, and then go fading among the tide, the man working the twine as he has, and will, only severing his eyes from the netting, his hands still performing the rhythm, to see the roar of helicopters come overwhelming the sky, the pairs of them not dividing but continuing in formation, even on reaching the surf, as they veer toward the rocks by the bluff, away from the light and into the world somehow bettered by the alchemy of the dawn.

Bob

I TELL MYSELF it's okay—kicking back a little the first day on the job. First days are always about paperwork, getting set up with HR, waiting for access to special files, figuring out how to use the voicemail and the copier.

Right now a guy whose name I can't remember is parading me around, and we're stopping office by office so I can learn what everyone's title is. He looks like a Stu or Stan, but I'm pretty sure neither of those is his name.

"Real quick, this is Barry, our new regional Head of Data Strategy. He just transferred from New York and'll be working in Jan's old office. Barry likes bananas; his favorite color is taupe; and he's all about CrossFit."

"Nice to meet you, Barry."

"Likewise."

A silence ensues now that we are off script, but before either of us is able to cleverly fill the gap, the woman, my new coworker, begins somewhat sheepishly:

"Say, I hope you don't mind . . . someone said you were the son of Henry Hamlin?"

"Henry Hamlin's son?"

"Someone would not be a liar," I say.

I had actually expected this to come up earlier and was kind of annoyed when no one had brought it up, thought maybe they wanted to but didn't feel comfortable, were worried about embarrassing or offending me by broaching the subject, and thought, Okay, let's just get it over with, you guys—isn't that what first days are really for?—though now that it's out in the open, I kind of wish we could go back to pretending.

"So," she grins, "what is it like? What is it like to be the son of Henry Hamlin?"

I've been asked this all my life. After years of disappointing them, I finally alighted on the only perfect response.

"It's about like what you think."

We stop by the breakroom. I am shown how to use the coffeemaker. It has been agreed as an informal policy that we are to discard the pods after use. We stop by the mailroom, where I am introduced to other strangers going to and fro, seeking their livelihoods, grateful there is that grace period of unaccountability in which I can count on being reminded whom everyone is, blameless albeit ignorant.

"Oh, look, you already have some mail."

In my mailbox is a large manila envelope from CCS.

After Stan or whoever has finished taking me on the rounds, in an effort not to appear idle, I open my piece of mail. As part of my onboarding, Imprimature has outsourced its wellness programs to Creative Counseling Solutions, and I am expected to answer the questionnaire honestly, to the best of my abilities. There are the usual questions (name, DOB, social, mailing address, etc.) before an onslaught of multiple choice, fill in the blank, true or false, inkblots I am instructed to provide a label for, some of them deliberately rather dark.

Do you ever lie to yourself?

How often do you have erotic thoughts? Select one range of the following . . .

THE SUMMER WE ATE OFF THE CHINA

The hamster eats its own _____

Within the last twenty-four hours have you wished you yourself or someone close to you did not exist?

At three o'clock I'm still at work.
"Already buried in paperwork?" says the guy.
"Filling out these forms for CCS."
"Have you gotten through to the server?"
"I haven't had a minute to check."
"Well, holler if you're still having issues."
Finally I come to the end. All my new colleagues minus a few have gone home for the night and an older man in a jumpsuit is going office by office and turning the lights on and emptying the trash before turning the lights back off and moving on. I sign and date the document and pack my things and place the forms in the self-addressed envelope and slip them in with tomorrow's outgoing stuff.

Our new apartment isn't too long a walk from my office on K Street. When Tori first came down in January, everyone had sold her on the idea that Adams Morgan is just like the West Village, only at a fraction of the cost, but in my opinion anywhere on the other side of the Hudson feels like slumming. A few of her paintings had appeared in a small gallery, drawing some attention. Then the owner invited her to be part of the summer show.
"In the City we're small fish, but down there, it's like we've paid our dues—we're at the top of the food chain."
So down we moved.
Many a night have I come home to find my partner besmocked and up to the elbows in color, absorbed in the miracle of creating. Once she had a paintball gun and was pelleting with orange and

red shot a portrait she'd done of Bush Senior. Not long ago I walked in, stepping over a floor draped wall to wall in tarp, and found Tori urinating over canvases she'd had washed in monoclonal antibodies, all in the name of art. Tonight I find her sitting on the sofa, the apartment still a mess of luggage, boxes against the wall. She has just stepped out of the shower, her hair slick with gel in a shiny integument, and she is smoking a cigarette from a platinum holder, a habit she acquired upon moving to DC.

After setting down my things, I position myself in a wallsit.

"How was it?"

"It was okay."

"How were they, the other office rats?"

Unlike myself, Tori was gifted a trust fund at the ripe age of sixteen and, depending on the nature of her audience, refers to her art as a "hobby," "trade," "job," "profession," or "calling."

"Some guy in need of a breath mint and what appeared to be a polyester suit gave me the tour. I think we're becoming chums."

I watch her look at her watch, a present from her last birthday.

"Toni is picking me up."

Toni—that is, Toni Cannelloni—is the owner of the gallery that is showing Tori's art. Half-Sicilian and one hundred percent out and proud, Toni has been insinuating that he's considering asking Tori to be his partner; therefore it is essential that she and Toni spend as much time and money together as possible.

"Don't wait up."

I watch her rise from the couch and snuff her cigarette in the ashtray sculpted in the fashion of a Henry Moore, on the completion of which feat she comes over and kisses me on the forehead like my mother has done.

After she leaves, the fumes from her cigarette still hover over the room. Vague wisps, attenuating tentacles, drifting toward the vent. The only clue that words have been spoken. The effect of which is to suggest something of a church after hours. Eventually I let myself stand and eat something.

A few days later the office manager stops me before I can cross his desk and tells me I have a visitor.

"Your eight-thirty's here."

"I don't have an eighty-thirty."

"He's in the green room. It's Bob Brody from CCS."

Through the window I see a man sitting alone at the conference table.

"Good morning." I enter the room. "Can I help you with something?"

He rises, and the two of us shake hands. He lowers himself into his chair, timing it as I sit. Not only are his beard and perm forty years out of date, but his crimson turtleneck and toast-colored corduroy suit put him in the camp of the keenest of vintage-store shoppers.

"Why you must be Mr. Barry," he says, half smiling. "You're exactly how I imagined you. You won't have to lose but a moment of your day."

"They said you're with CCS."

"I am—one of the tried and true—who not only believes in the value of what we do but insists on the overlap, the so-called butterfly effect, of our mutual vocations. You see, at CCS we're committed to providing our clients with the utmost care and support. But before we can commence with assembling a package of our individualized wellness offerings . . . well, let's just say some of your results came back a little bit unorthodox. But, if I may be so bold, I always welcome the thrill of a challenge."

I feel like we've met somewhere—very familiar he seems. His voice, soft and nearly a whisper, is like a polyester blanket, and it's difficult to tell whether he's being patronizing or altogether mocking me, or if that is just who he is—avuncular, yet slightly pedophiliac.

"What can I do for you exactly?"

"Not what you can do for me, Mr. Barry: what I can do for you. Your work is trying enough that contributing any more stress or uncertainty is the furthest of my concerns. Only based on the information you provided . . . well, let's just say you're a little bit of a niche man—a niche man, that is, like myself."

"What information?"

"I mean at CCS we've never seen anyone along your likes before. You're a hard nut to crack, if you'll pardon the cliché." All this while he has not stopped smiling, his eyes warm and twinkling, as though he himself were enamored by that glimmer of an accent, that soothing, agreeable hint of a drawl that suggests years of nourishing from goodwill casseroles and sweet tea by the quartload.

"Are you saying I did something wrong?"

"Quite the contrary. Your answers merely failed to account for one of our most important constituent indicators—a sense of motivation—thereby rendering our job a little more difficult in selecting which of our programs we like to pride ourselves in offering our clients."

"Like what kinds of programs?"

"Gosh, it seems like we have our hands in just about everything these days: diet, as in food delivery from our producers straight to your door; mindfulness seminars, retreats; deep tissue massage and acupuncture; binaural beat therapy; reiki; guided meditation; nature walks; survival skills; skydiving—you name it, we probably do it."

"All of that sounds nice, but frankly I'm too busy right now to even consider taking some sort of time off."

His smile expands so I can see the tips of his eyeteeth.

"Mr. Barry, I appreciate your candor. For the meantime perhaps you can be so kind as to help us simply by clarifying a paradox that left me and my colleagues ... well, boggled, to say the least."

"What kind of paradox?"

He has my questionnaire on the table and the page open to the part that he then indicates with a thick, pink finger. Even in his seriousness he seems somewhat amused.

"On question sixty-two: *I value my achievements as they may be seen in the eyes of my* blank, you answered by supplying the word *peers*. Then on sixty-three—the very next question, you see, Mr. Barry—in response to: *I hold the highest regard for the praise I have hoped to receive from my*, you wrote: *father*."

I nod, see no point in disagreeing.

"You understand how those are distinctly divergent answers for what is nearly the same prompt, and I noted a similar trend of inconsistency throughout your entire report."

"Are you saying I completed it wrong?"

He almost lets himself chuckle. "Don't worry: you're not going to have to retake anything. You're just making us earn our keep." Unprompted, he gathers the papers and stands.

"I won't waste any more of your time. I'm glad we've had this occasion to meet. I expect we'll be in touch quite soon with your offerings. By the way, in which direction would be the washroom?"

I motion the way down the hall.

"Again," I follow him to the door, which he opens and ushers me through with what I assume must be a kind of reflexive politeness, "unfortunately these days I'm so buried in work that I doubt

I'll be using your services. Maybe down the road. Thank you for stopping by, Mr. Brody."

"Bob," he says. "Just Bob."

"Bob!" I was standing on the corner of K and 15th, when whom should I spot on the corner opposite but the man himself, the person who'd been in the back of my thoughts.

He looks up out of his daydream. I sense he immediately recognizes me, for a smile breaks open that too solid face. I'll wait here, he motions.

"Mr. Barry!" he says on my reaching him. "Why what a very pleasant surprise. You're not working so late, which must be a relief."

"What are you doing right now?"

Based on his reaction, I realize what I said was uncouth.

"No, I mean, I'm out to the bar at the Hay-Adams before I turn in for the night, and I wanted to offer to buy you a drink. If you like, we can discuss my conscience or whatever."

For just an instant I detect the passing of a frown. Then he is himself—dauntless, happy, blithe.

"Under usual sets of circumstances I prefer to keep my interactions with clients to as professional a setting as possible. But for you, Mr. Barry, okay."

Instead of the Hay-Adams, he guides me to a place up the street—almost a dive I'd call it—that I would have never pegged him to haunt.

"From my days as a reporter," he explains. "The Post was our favorite watering hole. Many of us hacks left our razor and strap in the washroom. I told you I was a niche man, just like yourself. Before companies likes CCS came along, your options for self-care were . . . well, shall we say, somewhat limited. It usually came at the end of a long day in the form of a rocks glass with an ounce of liquor." Nevertheless he had insisted on ordering an orange juice.

"You weren't always with CCS?"

"I've been a lot of things, Mr. Barry: a newshound, a mechanic, believe it or not I taught third grade. For a while I worked in broadcast. Then I went back to school and struck out with my own practice, but . . ." His voice drifts. Not once has it deviated from that saccharine equanimity with its trace of upbringing in the Deep South all but pummeled out and that ever-present mocking or overly sympathetic quality that I have almost come to ignore. "Let's just say that going corporate has allowed me to maintain a certain distance that enables me to endure."

"No," I say, three gimlets in, "I get it. Burnout is a real problem. When I actually stop and reflect on the number of hours I've clocked . . . I think I should be a genius or something. If I could go back in time and tell myself how much . . . I don't believe I'd do it."

He smiles, nods like a bobblehead, confirming, encouraging my words despite any hesitancy, understanding, acknowledging pain.

"Maybe I'd work on a ranch or something."

"Mr. Barry, at the risk of being gauche by resuming our discussion of earlier in the midst of a friendly outing, I would like to remind you that this is precisely what we detected in your results. I think we're getting to the heart of something."

"What's that?"

"Why a question of motivation, Mr. Barry. A question of why you're dragging yourself out of bed and into your penny loafers every morning and not saying, 'To heck with it,' of why bother in the first place. Don't you feel what I mean?"

I do know what he means. As a personal rule, for years I haven't bothered to let myself question why it is I am doing what it is I am doing. If I had to stop and think, if I ever had to sit still, it was always to consider the next move, what the next task at hand should be. Go to school, earn a degree, find a woman, make more money, have a family that took nice vacations somewhere.

"Doesn't the world need people who work?"

This whole time he has scarcely taken his eyes off me; he seems to be considering my every gesture, weighing my tone and diction, and noting it all in some mental file.

"Mr. Barry, do you ever watch the History Channel?"

"Like I said, I don't have time these days to watch TV."

"Frankly neither do I, but if you'll bear with me for a moment, I kindly believe you'll see where all this is headed. Anyway, my life partner and I are great fans of the History Channel. We love learning all we can about history. History . . . it's a fascinating subject. It's funny, when you think about it, the whole learning of history . . . why that could take up an eternity in itself. So I guess they're right about what they say about us being doomed to repeat everything. Doesn't seem like there's much way around it, or really much of a choice. Where was I? Oh yes, the documentary. So me and my life partner Jessie one night were watching this special they were doing on the Golden Gate Bridge. Told all about how it was built in the middle of the Great Depression when America was struggling, really fighting to make ends meet. How Franklin Delano Roosevelt was so smitten with the idea of a big old golden bridge stretching out across the bay like a symbol to the folks going through hard times that he went and hired a fancy architect to come all the way over from Paris to design the thing. But when they got around to today and the facts and figures of running it, the upkeep and the maintenance—really fascinating stuff—they talked to a guy, a fella by the name of Mr. Jorge Hernandez. Mr. Jorge spends three hundred and sixty of three hundred and sixty-five days every year strapped to a powerful harness, painting the bridge top to bottom. At which rate it takes him a little over five years effectively to do the job. He paints one side; then he comes back and he paints the other. And do you know what his answer was when they asked him what he does then, once he's through with painting the bridge? 'What do you do after you finish painting the Golden Gate Bridge, Mr. Jorge?' is how they put it to him, the question. Well, Mr. Jorge, he just stood there and looked straight there toward that camera. Then finally he just shrugged. 'I start painting it again.' He turns around and starts right back. 'I start painting it again!' Jessie and I nearly fell out of our seats."

Bob shakes his head, perhaps as yet from disbelief or perhaps out of profound gratitude for all the workers the world over who are doing such thankless tasks.

"I believe there's a lesson to be learned there, Mr. Barry. I believe there's a mighty good lesson."

At nights I come back to a space where Tori's presence is indicated by a few telling disruptions—some new cigarettes crammed in the ashtray, some food removed from the fridge, some fresh paintings against the wall, the smell of smoke and perfume—but other than that it is like we are living with different ghosts. Now and then, just as I am leaving, she returns after her nights on the town with Toni, whose nude abstractions, I read, are becoming the talk of Mass Ave Heights, and there, in the pale of early dawn, we stare at each other, silent, unconvinced of our senses' reality, she in a smear of mascara, myself in a tracksuit with briefcase, shoes, and lunch, afraid that any word might shatter the illusion of the other's immateriality, as a courtesy passing on.

I do not run into Bob, nor do I dwell on him—I am in the thralldom of deadlines, reviews, reports, conferences, meetings, crunching the numbers—though it would be wrong to claim that Bob is not on my mind. For in the spare hours I allow myself to sleep he appears like a cancer in the corridors of my unconscious. Undeniable, yet strangely benign. I am riding through a quiet blue prairie, my destiny to found some bastion of peace, when a wind comes up and who should overtake me at a gallop and with a courteous tip of the hat but Bob. Or in the agony of ascension, beard weighted down by pounds of snow, in the azure of near-outer space, who is it who is already seated there atop the pinnacle, a smile as blithe and dauntless as though he were just gifted a sweater by his favorite aunt, but Bob. Bob in the funhouse, Bob in the jungle. Bob in the Great Bed of Ware, below the Blarney Stone, striding the backdrops of innocent memory, among the black wastes of moorless waters that stretch on forever and on. Bob, Bob, Bob.

One day, out of the blue, I get a message:

Dear Mr. Barry,

It is with great and deferential apologies that I write you concerning the status of your wellness offerings. Of late my colleagues and I have experienced some heavy turnaround in light of the recent change in our administration. Rest assured your materials are in capable and well-meaning hands.

Yours truly,

Bob

The doorknob rattles to life. My first thought: an intruder. But who is it but Tori.

Strange, it's not even midnight.

She catches me holding a plank.

"Where's Toni?"

She throws down a purse and takes off a cardigan and lets it drop.

"Toni's in South Dakota buying a cockatoo."

"If he can wait, the parade's in another week."

She has that look on her face that says she wants me to know she is not going to let herself be annoyed.

"Freud was wrong," she delivers this to the ground. "Men are the ones who have penis envy."

After she goes to bed, I scavenge the boxes stacked against the wall, signifying the status quo that we are not yet ready for domestic calm or wholly accustomed to the idea of our move, until I find the one with her books. I take out a random volume and flip to a random page and read a random sentence: *Leonardo often employed the techniques of sfumato and aria grossa, of rendering a hazy, indistinct background in order to heighten the impressions of his subjects, such as in the classic case of La Joconde.*

Instead of following her to bed, I make myself jog through the city. Nearly everywhere I run I can make out the Washington Monument. Aglow in a soft chalky light. Peeking out over buildings, between alleys, over roads. I jog up the Mall, up the steps of the Capitol, and around the reflecting pool, eventually right to the base, craning my neck at the pale raised finger of democracy.

Maybe, I think, Tori is right.

Pop of uncorked champagne. Chatter and chaffering. The sexual throb and confidence of jazz on a hot summer night. Someone has dropped a glass. The gallery is lined wall to wall with canvases, some of which I recognize but none of which I can claim to understand.

"He's out-Pollocked Pollock!"

"It's an experience, not a depiction."

I go up to one very close.

Ahimsa in White. The one beside it, *A Schadenfreude in Gray. Wisdom, Plm of the Lft Hnd.* None look like anything. A rorschach for making out splatters. Something a kid with half a brain could paint.

Over by the wall stands Tori, her hair piled up in the style of Nefertiti. She is wearing a sleeveless red cocktail gown that is the only pleasing referent in the room.

Time and again she has averred that she despises mingling with "artsy" types—what I assumed was for her like gazing in a brightly lit mirror—a statement that I took to be fact until the day I overheard her say just the opposite, that she feels like a fish out of water when rubbing elbows with the bourgeoisie.

"Yes, the Italians are important painters."

"Why are they important?" I cut in.

"Not *important*," laughs Tori, showing her tonsils, "*importing*. They're importing them, the Italians, painters."

"That is if you can stand living without wi-fi and being smooched by all manner of canaille, then you should definitely take up the Baronessa Monti. By all means expatriate!"

"Maybe we should move to Tuscany?"

"Which one's Toni?" I whisper.

"Toni came down with a cold," says a man who overheard me.

"Poor thing!" hoots another.

"Yes, what a sensitive little prick!"

"But seriously, I think that's the appeal of what you're doing. To the Tuscans, they'll seem Tuscan. To the Chinese, they'll be Chinese. In the West, they strike us as Occident. To connoisseurs, they're a blast of fresh air. And to the mob . . . well, if you'll excuse me the phrase, they'll be *merde*."

"I like this one's sfumato," I say. With my glass I motion to the canvas behind us and gesture toward drizzles. "What do you guys think of this one's sfumato?"

Everyone is looking at me, not at the painting; perhaps they believe I'm drunk, but I am not drunk but stone-cold sober. Casually, the group of them uproots. I watch them drift like a tumbleweed to the other side of the gallery. Only a young professional in a goober-alert haircut is the last to linger in my orbit. He smiles. The smile is mocking and sympathetic, and for a second I want to ask him if he has met Bob.

"The cheese stands alone," he winks. Then he too leaves for somewhere, something.

On my coming out of a meeting, the office manager catches me by the arm. "Your eleven o'clock's here. He said you were meeting in your office."

I have no eleven o'clock. And sure enough, there with his back to me in his dated corduroy suit sits Bob. He rises, eager to shake my hand, that air of patronage or unwholesome sympathy creeping at the edge of his smile. There are so many questions I have wanted to ask him, ideas I'd like his input on, but for the time being all I can say is, "We don't have a meeting today, Bob. You lied to our secretary. Now what is it you want?"

"Mr. Barry, my oh my, are you looking quite trig and filling out that merino suit, which leads me to believe you are in fact finding some downtime in which to attend to your personal fitness. Regarding the unscheduled nature of my visit, which really is inexcusable, I trust you'll shortly agree that the confidential precautions I took, and which the matter of my visit presumes . . . well, let's just say I wanted to keep this as quiet for you as possible."

"What exactly do you mean?"

"Why Mr. Barry," he beams, "the makeup of your report. Surely you'd think by now we'd have offered you our amenities if the issue didn't lie with yourself."

"What issue are you referring to?"

"Yes, it's important to be clear as possible." He takes from his battered briefcase that looks too dingy for even a third-rate thrift store to accept in good conscience what I see are the documents I filled out on my first day of work and flips to a certain page, indicating the question with the tap of his finger. "To question 93b: *Have you ever experienced violent or untoward thoughts concerning a paternalistic figure?* you responded, *Yes*, an answer that naturally gave us some pause, causing us to follow up with the Suffolk County Police. And while, as I'm sure you have already been well informed, there are no criminal records concerning your precise person, we did find your case to be . . . well—how shall we say?—very interesting, to say the least. By the way, I must compliment you, Mr. Barry: what a wonderful little ficus tree you have. My dentist has one just like it in his waiting room."

"What are you getting at, Bob?"

"Nothing that is not already evident to the public and what I presume is your remembrance. That, although no charges were ever filed against your person, thus rendering you ultimately unconvicted, given the extreme, shall we say, oddity of the situation, you, a Mr. Barry, were named the sole, lone-acting perpetrator, who discharged a powerful firearm at a Mr. Henry Hamlin, an action whose consequence resulted in the paralysis of the victim's upper-left arm and, as the records indicate now at the court of probate, likely resulted in your removal from the said victim's will."

"Look, it was an accident. I made a mistake while we were out hunting pheasant. I don't see what any of these things have to do with how you and I go about doing our jobs."

"But, Mr. Barry, this has everything to do with your position as Head of Data Strategy in a *Fortune* 500 company such as Imprimature. As you and I discussed in our talk of earlier, motivation is always key."

That tranquil demeanor and gentle timber—I may as well have been sitting across from the eye of a category-five hurricane. To my best judgment he appears to want nothing at all, simply to be at peace.

"What do you want?"

He chuckles, delighted perhaps by my naiveté or that I should be so thoughtful as to inquire about him.

"Why only your well-being of course, Mr. Barry. To see you actualized and spread your wings. To know you have followed and attained your bliss. By the way, remind me: In which direction would be your washroom? I seem to have a mote lodged in my eye that makes blinking for the moment rather cumbersome."

"I'm going to see Don about this," I say, rising. "I'm going to lodge a complaint against Creative Counseling Services—"

"Solutions."

"—and I'm going to recommend Imprimature terminate its contract with your company. I'm going to argue our meetings have bordered on outright harassment."

"Mr. Barry, you of all people should know that conviction does not equal truth. Moreover, rest assured I have already spoken at length with our mutual contact about your circumstances, and he has offered me his word of honor—"

"No, now you come with me."

I am out of the office and down the hall, and before I can think I should knock, I have interrupted Don in a meeting.

"Barry, excuse me, you'll have to—"

"Don, what the hell are we doing doing business with these jokers at CCS? This guy Bob . . . he's been borderline close to harassing me ever since the first day!"

"Bob?" says Don, a blinking mask of authority. "Bob? From CCS?" He turns to the two men at the table. "Gentlemen, excuse us for a second. Barry, if you could please lower your voice—"

"No, to hell with this, Don. Any company that thinks it can outsource to CCS makes me sick! Count me out! I'm through!"

On turning around, having assumed that Bob was right there beside me throughout my big scene, I am perplexed to discover he has not followed me but remained behind in my office, in the chair in my office. But he is not in my office. I check the washroom: nor is he there either.

"Where did he go?" I question the office manager.

"Who?"

"That guy, the man in the funny suit. Bob from CCS. He took the stairs or the elevator?"

"I have no idea what you're talking about."

Down on the street I expect to spot him hailing a cab or by the curb waiting for the bus, but there is no one on the sidewalk, only shadows of strangers' likenesses going about their days. I start toward home, realize I have left some stuff in my desk. I tell myself I am moving back to New York, where things make sense, and if Tori is resistant, then maybe we'll live apart, that staying in DC for the sake of Tori's arts and crafts projects is not worth the mental toll it's been taking and the strain on our relationship. My phone starts to ring.

"Yes?"

"Is this Barry?"

"Who is this?"

"Right, it's Toni. Tori and I are at my place, Barry. She's been posing for me all morning. There's something she wants to say." Toni's voice sounds not at all how I imagined.

"Put her on the phone."

"Why don't you come over and the three of us can chat. I'm at 62 Y."

The cab drops me off in front of a brutalist concrete townhouse. At the driveway I get buzzed in. Through the door I am able to see past myself down a hall: a white plaster corridor with frames spaced formally along the walls. Stark fluorescent lighting. I knock several times. No one appears.

At last I try the knob. The door is unlocked, and I let myself open it. Inside all is quiet except for the squawking of a bird. Only my footsteps are there to contradict me. Though I am sure every piece of artwork is priceless, none of it looks like anything—just colors, stains, and swirls. Above me abides a cockatoo in its cage. I go up the stairs, up to a gallery of more paintings. A light is on amid a cloud of smoky humidity, though before I can enter it, out walks Tori with her hair in a wrap, in a bathrobe. Both of us start.

"Oh my god, Barry! You literally gave me a heart attack. What are you doing here?"

"What am I doing here! What are you doing here? You're the one who's been posing all day in the nude!"

"Who told you I was naked?"

"He kisseth first, then sits at blithe to eat." I turn around and who is regarding us but Bob like a thief in the night. In lieu of the corduroy suit and perm, he is wearing glasses and crowned by a Warholesque wig, and he is muffled in a fur coat far too hot for this time of year in DC.

"Bob!"

"Barry, this is Toni. Toni offered me a partnership in the gallery. We were drinking champagne, and I took a shower."

"Pardon, I was stuck in the loo, though I see you found your way in."

"The washroom?"

"Clever." He watches me with the look of someone who has achieved clarity by an act of mere will.

"This is the man from work who's been hounding me ever since my first day on the job!" I tell this to Tori, who only stares, who has scarcely taken her eyes off Bob.

"She said," says Bob, "and I quote: 'My partner uses work as a straitjacket for his neuroses.' Didn't you say that, my chuckling?"

There is something about his voice—Toni's voice or Bob's—that is as far off from Bob's as can be. Different yet strangely familiar.

"Always buried under work," says Bob. "Under deadlines and pointless meetings. Barely a second for anything but his three-mile jog and his acai berry healthshake. My boy, you're running away from the point that your life doesn't mean anything. If he could only look at the paintings."

I know what his voice sounds like: it sounds just like me! Not an imitation, but a counterfeit to the breath.

"Bob," I say, "you're sick. Why are you doing this?"

"Why does he keep saying 'Bob'?" says Tori.

The cockatoo resumes its squawking. "Bob!"

"Yes, why do you keep saying 'Bob'?" says Bob. The two of us continue to stare. "Ah, his silence is so accurate. Perhaps after all he's ready to deny everything."

With that I lunge toward him, grabbing him by the mink and the two of us tumble to the floor. I hear a frame come crashing down beside us, the cage, the bird screeching, flapping its wings. Tori screams. "I'm calling the police!"

"You are Bob!" I'm on top of him, beating his face. After a while he quits resisting. "Bob!" I say. "Bob! Bob!"

Soon he looks unrecognizable, but even once they pull us apart, I am still saying his name. Am saying it still.

Bob. Bob. Bob.

Tauroctony

THAT'S WHY I MAKE THEM CRY!

So bellowed the Bull King
Unleashed the wrath of his terror

The earth thrown into . . .
. . . fire of the Roaring One!
Tumult rent the hearts of the sons of . . .
. . . everything torn by flame!
Sounds burning . . . eyes . . .

Ash . . . oo . . . ting
. . . gluts his rage on numbers slain
Rending and tearing . . .
. . . ribs and cloven hands . . .

Bodies cleft . . .
. . . left . . .
. . . the sons of the Ammonites torn in half

THAT'S WHY I MAKE THEM CRY!

Awake, Hepidore!
Awake, son of Chance and Determination!
for we have arrived at the Isle of Meer

THE SUMMER WE ATE OFF THE CHINA

A lone flier yelled
Vyadha the thunderbird fluttering in the lamp of the ether

Hepidore woke
He woke to the cry of the thunderbird
Woke in the hull of a dinghy whose sail was wind in the hair of
        maidens
The waves shouting with cutwater before the ship
Woke with the keel smarting against his back

Echoes of the Bull King thundering through a gray sea

Hepidore sat
He sat up and looked about
Saw cyclones ravaging the horizon
Powered by the rage of the Bull King
For his ways are also in whirlwinds
He raises the dust and turns the clouds black

Shut up, pea brain!
I know where we are!

Before them an island of dark matter
An island of jawless skulls
A scree of charred eyeless skulls
Leading up a sharp steep of skulls
At the top bleached white, the color of shells
some rotten and crumbled to dust
Others the color of ash

TAUROCTONY

The boat ran ashore
Hepidore left the ship
Lept to the Isle of Meer
Left the gaze of the maidens, brushed their long strings of hair
Hepidore left the boat and did not look back

He followed the thunderbird Vyadha
Clambered to the summit of Meer
At the top he spied Egel guarding the entrance
He climbed the summit of skulls
The thunderbird flew round the boy

Egel the hermit stood as still as a rock
Unmoved were hands, feet, and tongue

There seemed a speech about the air

Speak!

I wish to challenge the Bull King! cried Hepidore
I seek the means to defeat the Bull King!

No one can grasp him, replied the hermit
But his grasp is over all seeing
He is beyond all fathoming
Yet he is fathomed in all things

Answer me, replied the hermit
and you shall have the Golden Spear
by which you shall kill the Bull King

I grow from this, from here I learn of love
You pursue me even once I leave

THE SUMMER WE ATE OFF THE CHINA

Hepidore searched the passages of his brain
He searched his mind's many nooks and crinks
He scoured the manifold channels
Overthrew the tables of memory
He thought and came up wanting

A shell, said Hepidore
A snail shell, said the son of Chance and Determination

That is unacceptable, said the hermit
Clearly the answer is home

Hepidore sank in despair
His heart sank to his stomach
Vyadha the thunderbird sank to the ground
Unmoved, the old hermit watched them
For so long they had lived on air

It is your wish to avenge yourself on the Roaring One
but this cannot be done without the Golden Spear
Hence all who meet the Bull King must die
And every soul shall have a taste of death

Tell me, said Egel the hermit
Speak, for your gaze pulls at the strings of my heart
Do you hate your brothers and sisters?
The hermit eyed the boy to the quick

Because of eating so little the limbs were like vine
Because of eating so little the spine stood forth like yarn
The skin was not black, brown, or gold, but translucent top to toe

I have no family, said Hepidore
The Bull King has undone my past

Hearing these things, the hermit's heart hurt
The hermit clutching that robe of rags

And yet the dead do not live
And the living do not die

Very well
You shall not have the Golden Spear
but I shall give you the Skates of Unsolving

It is your wish to take vengeance on the Roaring One
but this cannot be except through the spear

Hence all who meet the Bull King must die
And every soul shall have a taste of the death we mention

The skates shall help you skate through the Maze of Ice
It is the Maze of Ice that keeps the Bull King!

Egel the hermit rose from a puddle of rain
Egel the hermit wore a robe made of rags
Veins showing over the body
Showed them the path to the cave
Led them to the vast pit of ice

Hepidore left the Isle of Meer and descended
Hepidore and Vyadha . . .

. . .
. . . no graceful shelter
. . . darkness enlightened the cave
Death . . .

THAT'S WHY I MAKE THEM CRY!
THAT'S WHY I MAKE THEM CRY!

THE SUMMER WE ATE OFF THE CHINA

The Bull King's bellows redounded against the ice
Froze the cave to its core

Hepidore stood there quite frozen

Awake, Hepidore!
Awake, son of Chance and Determination!
For we have arrived at the Maze of Ice
From the breath of the Bull King comes the ice
Chasms measureless to fathom
Floors and walls, a terrible maze!

Hepidore looked about in the dark light of the cave
He squinted through the palpable dark
He studied the walls of ice
Examined the hardened floor
Saw ripples spread throughout the frozen stream
Ripples of frozen time
The screams of the Roaring One preserved in ice!
And yet his raging is also of fire, his breath the work of death

Shut up, pea brain!
I know where we are!

Hepidore donned the sharp Skates of Pain
He laced the strings and began to glide
The thunderbird flew overhead
Sped through a great uncertainty of winding ways
They meandered through the maze of the Bull King

Hepidore raced a league of the Maze of Ice
Then he raced another
He continued turning left
The thunderbird scouting and hooting
Hepidore skated until his breath was cold
He skated until his skin was coated with ice

How close? cried Hepidore
We are still many years of leagues away from the Bull King, said
    Vyadha

Hepidore raced two leagues of the Maze of Ice
Then he raced three and five
He continued turning left
The thunderbird scouting and hooting
Hepidore skated until his breath was crystal
skated until his skin was covered with a layer of ice

How close? cried Hepidore
We are still many years of leagues away from the center

Hepidore raced eight leagues
Then he raced thirteen and twenty-one
He continued turning left
The thunderbird scouting and hooting
Hepidore skated until his breath was solid
skated until his skin was loaded with ice

The Maze of Ice goes on forever!
At this rate my grandchildren will never reach the Bull King!

Hepidore sank in despair
His heart sank to his stomach
Vyadha sank toward the ground
For so long he had lived in the air

Look, said the thunderbird
Can you not see?
Are you unable to discriminate?
Here is a place to break through!
Here is a place of weakening!

So yelled the lone flier
Pointed at the wall of ice

Hepidore pushed through the ice wall
He broke a path through the maze
He skated thirty-four leagues
... broke ...

... weakening!
...

Hepidore ...
... the ice

THAT'S WHY I MAKE THEM CRY!

The roar of the Bull King shook the great maze
His bellow shattered the walls, divided the passages

THAT'S WHY I MAKE THEM CRY!

TAUROCTONY

Farther he could not go
Beyond all was back
Hepidore entered the gateway to all mystery

Wake, Hepidore!
Turn round!
The Bull King waits there behind you!

Hepidore registered the presence behind him
turned and regarded the Bull King

The Bull King sat on his Throne of Power
under a vague mist of death
Somewhere where light and dark never mingle

His eyes were like burning coals
On his head reclined a crown of flames
His maw was greased with blood

His eyes seared what they looked on, looked on with secret
    knowledge
On his head were many sharp horns
His dewlaps ghastly in their gore
Whatever he touches he shall sever and make but as dust!

THAT'S WHY I MAKE THEM CRY!

He bellowed his bellow of terror!
The keeper of the maze snorting and raging!

THEY CRY!
THEY CRY!
THEY CRY!

THE SUMMER WE ATE OFF THE CHINA

My limbs fail me, cried Hepidore
My throat is parched
My body trembles
My hair stands on end

At that the Roaring One took up the thunderbird
He tore off the white blades of his wings
He tossed the bird like a ball

The Bull King snorted and a pit opened
A chasm of bottomless ice

My head is spinning, said Vyadha
Everything is moving
Accomplish your end with diligence

And died

I loved the thunderbird!
A halcyon among hoopoes!
But you struck him and broke off his wings!

Hepidore grabbed the bull by the horns
The son of Chance and Determination wrestled the fearful king

They grappled each other, holding like wrestlers
They shattered the walls and floor
Toppled the great Maze of Ice

Endless the flow of energy!
Exhaustless the exchange of blows!

TAUROCTONY

The Roaring One clasped him and began to pry
Hepidore felt his limbs and insides dividing
His heart fell to his stomach
Sounds were burning, his eyes were burning
Hepidore himself became a thing of flame

He looked the bull in the eyes

With a twist of his skates he severed the Roaring One!
With a twist of his ankles the Roaring One became undone!

The Bull King bellowed a bellow that trembled the globe on its
    axis
left Hepidore on his bed of snow

A black hole unfolded between his legs
A labyrinth of organs spilled onto the ice
Blind with pain, the white ox fell
toppled, whimpered, and died

Quiet the maze
Quiet the chasms
Quiet the place of all mystery
as darkness descended to light

The peace of nothing settled over the maze
Silence followed by whispers
Whispers followed by shouts of ice in its cracking and breaking

The ice began to melt
The ripples to quiver and wave

THE SUMMER WE ATE OFF THE CHINA

Pain overwhelmed the body of Hepidore
Broken the whole way through
He was not long for that world

He lay down and rested his curls
The water felt cool to his throat
Over his mind and body a weakening

A chorus of cries joined him in his song

O let it come, let it come!
Whatever has been has been
O let it come, let it come!
Whatever will be will be
O let it come, let it come!
Whatever is must is

H . . . id . . . ing
. . . the lamp of ether
He spi . . . ruled . . .

. . . wake . . .
. . . cry

Dagonet

"And then Sir Dagonet the king's fool armed him in the shield and jesseraunce belonging to Sir Pigskin, and with his spear and scabbard he rode forth apace. And all the knights did marvel and make merry, and they were passing glad. And when Sir Anthrax soon espied Sir Dagonet riding forth in the guise of Sir Pigskin, he was mickle afeard; and wherefore he set forth his horse, rating Sir Dagonet as he were wood."

—Sir Thomas Malory, *Le Morte D'Arthur*

So THIS was the end. That's what all the headlines were saying. "The End for Arthur Eugene Dagonet!" For weeks a rumor had hung in the air like a bad stench in the pants of the cosmos, but this morning it had finally come bursting out, all guts, germs, grossness, everything—wet and whistling to the tune of and painting the picture in vivid excretion "The End of Dagonet!"

It had started with a woman. (For is that not how all stories blame their origin? Unless thou believest what came before the woman or the egg must needs be neither, but the fellow coming long ere the woman.) And this damsel, this slutty maiden, being carven to ensnare a good man's eye in the alluring contrapposto of Our Lady of So-Help-Me Tours while sporting the hefty bankbags from a heist of olden days, did lie in wait to catch her a fattened celebrity, and thereby knowing the lad in rut, did pounce upon his fancy. Did pounce upon the unerring truthfulness of his cock. Now it had hit the stands, making the headlines of all the newspapers, blogs, digital babble and chitchat and tweets by pernicious gander, forming the tattle of the talking heads, his own during which—obese, obscene, and oversized smile, the perfect profile of a proper predator—the effigy of a dead god not to be buried but spat upon and chunked to the turds of the East River to drifty far out to sea, where, bobbing, bloated, grotesquely bizarre, it might curl the lips of a passing dolphin in an affect of genuine hilarity and, even more improbably, wash up on the sands among the tribes of Jimbabawe, where he could hope to begin his comeback. Even Jersey was too good for him. "The End of Dagonet!" He was tasting the end all right. Downing marvelous mouthfuls of it (he who was so adept at spewing the shit from his mouth), of antimachismo menstrual murderous mayhem to boot, a siphon for the weeping women and toilet for all manner of clamorous clambaked claims. This was the end of Dagonet.

Thus he was cooking breakfast. Standing boxered and beerbellied and leering down at the slab of French toast (his dick minding its own business, thank you) after his usual morning wake and bake and half glass of raw gin and cognac jacuzzi, just trying to get through the damn day without eating two tubs of Alldone's ice cream for the upcoming drama with Meryl Streep for which he was contractually obliged to remain at two-forty and which by now had probably had him liposuctioned from the cast, replacing him with one of his less potent rivals who toted that thirty percent extra schlub and was deemed priapically innocuous, having been rubberstamped by the frigid lips of the Cult of Death. That was what was happening right now this second.

"BREAKFAST HAS BEEN SERVED!" he belted for the umpteenth time—or maybe he had screamed it in his head? It was just so typical. Culture needed a fat little porker for her annual *fête fachée*, and he was the piggywiggy who had managed to get stuck. He was paying his dues after living high on the hog, you could say. For a while there'd been signs his career was starting to flag, his ingenuity losing steam; he'd even been toying with the idea of retirement. Maybe he should take this as a sign for a career change? He could be a teller at the Santander (*"Sit on Santander Claus's lap and tell him what you'd like—he's always ready to make a deposit! Ho ho ho!"*) or a monk. Hide away in some select castle by the sea on a remote island where he could marinate his meat in tranquility and the media would never find him, only the monks. But they would find him, find him funny, ha! *"Let me tell you: It's not at all pleasant for me to be this egotistical and then be criticized for it. I make this look very easy!"*

"IS ANYBODY EVEN LISTENING?" he declaimed, thereupon stuffing the French toast he'd just finished burning, after waterboarding the bread in syrup, in one piece into his piehole.

The articles on the interwebs were saying she had never given him her consent. And yet he thought that when one so lucidly expressed, "May I taketh my dick *en plein air*?" and the answer a "sure, why not," an adult agreement had thereby been bandied in which one succumbed to the shedding of clothes. (Next time he'd call his lawyer and kindly request he administer a syringe of saltpeter directly into his dorsal vein.) Consent. What did that word even mean? A thing that women decide to give only contingent on whether they get to come? He was three inches too short for consent. *It was more an apology than an act of erotic aggression . . . does that make sense? How do you know when a woman gives you her consent? When she smiles at you while showing you the art of a* blowjob. No, I'd fuck my own ass if my dick could reach back there, to the asshole. No, seriously, I would do that. I'D ... DO ... ME! Already I do me all the time in point of fact. I'm my biggest hoe. We're very sexually active, he and I. We're willing to try new things. Only ... at the end of the day I wouldn't let him fuck me that way. Because gay-me never gave straight-me his consent for being a faggot.*

He thought: When Jane finds out about this she is going to have a field day, head cunt as she is for the hysterical Cult of Death. I wonder if she'll bring me to court for the terms of custody. Liar: You hope she does.

He patted the procumbent toast, a useless act done with the backside of the spatula, vaguely sexual in origin. Like consent.

I wonder, do we give them our consent? Am I in charge of being willing to enter into this sexual experience? I find that a very unsettling double standard. A very unsettling double standard. Which sounds precisely like what you call it when you're allowed to fuck your wife of ten years twice in a single night. Perhaps he should commit suicide. He'd been flirting with hanging himself only a few weeks earlier. It was supposed to feel quite good, asphyxiating while you came.

The phone rang. It was Dyson. Dagonet tried to complete chewing the last of the toast he was expanding into his waist, but his jaw was tired from masticating, so he was doing his best to savor it. He was as always so thoughtful when it came to his French toast.

"Gene? Hey, all I'm getting is noise."

"Thuuthz chthuzmeeting Frchthrust."

"Well, I hope you fucking choke on your French toast, my friend, because today is the day we're finally forcefed to swallow our balls, and no amount of Hail Marys or Pater Nosters are going to bring them back."

"I predict this will all blow over."

"You pre—"

"I mean, look, from the outset I've only considered two themes worthy of my act: penile feats and compassion. This shouldn't come as a huge surprise to anybody who cares."

"Oh, your coming is a very huge surprise to everybody, Gene," said Dyson in his guilty Catholic schoolboy voice. "You realize there's no pleasant way for me to spin this? You can't put a positive bent on this sort of trainwreck."

"By positive bent you mean—"

"Oh Christ, they're saying others are going to start coming forward now as a result. Do you know who they might be? Maybe there's still time we could buy them off."

"But, Dyson," protested Dagonet, slathering a new piece of toast in the batter of his inebriated making before flinging it onto the grillpan like a cumshaw of natural gratuity (he was outwardly quite calm and possessed), "if every time I asked for someone's consent before I was about to give them something I assumed they wanted, I'd just be asking all the time and never delivering. I'd be no funnier than your proctologist."

"Oh Christ, oh Christ, oh Christ," he was saying, likely at this moment packing his bag and dick up for the long exile ahead.

"You gotta believe—"

"You just don't get it, do you? You're like Rembrandt in the dark. These are very serious allegations of misconduct. This isn't just part of your brand."

"Let me stop you right there, old buddy. See, what does that even mean, 'misconduct'? As if *she's* fit to judge. I may conduct myself like Mother Teresa compared to Buffalo Bill. In fact I misconducted myself last night like I was leading the Trans-Siberian Orchestra with the remnant of a half-eaten turkey leg. Besides, it's like once you've been exposed to one, you've been exposed more or less to all. Kind of like Chinese people. So in a sense she should recognize that everyone's misconducted her. Only why does it have to be public? That's what I honestly don't get. Why does she have to accuse me this way before the entire world? If she wanted the cash, why not just ask? If she wanted to see me in jail, why not press charges or lead me inside a dogcrate? I've helped so many people along the way come up in this business—including, let's not forget, *her*—and they don't realize the mental toll it takes of trying to remain a star, of exposing your soul night after night, and this is the sole thanks I—"

"Let me be crystal clear with you, Gene: No one is thanking you for this. Me especially. Christ, I should have seen the writing on the wall years ago with that puppet-show girl, but then you'd tell me it was only randy graffiti in a bathroom stall. Well, let me be clear with you now, my friend: I am through with keeping your hands clean. This is my resignation. I quit, Gene. I'm sorry, but—wait . . . if anybody, I'm the one who deserves an apology. I'm completely finished with you, you asshole!"

Thereupon our comic, our tragic comic, our white male upper-class sissily genendered tragicocomicasaurus, levied from his band of dramatis personae his most flamboyant Yid, whom he referred to as Mr. Bagel, stoutly against the microphone and matched him fervor for fervor:

"But, Dyson, the comeback tour *is* my apology! You'll see, I'll lay it all out and the goyim will understand! Shylock will have his moneys! I'll even throw in a few spare pounds of flesh. You can pick any area you like, only please spare me my junk. Besides it's unkosher it is, the porker." Modulating to normal. "It'll be a funny sort of *Mein Kampf*. Hello? Dyson, are you with me?"

Dead air. Curtain. He was playing to an empty house.

"HEEELLLLLLLLO?"

"If you were going to be so anal, why did you wake us up so late? I just got out of the bath."

Enter stage left his elder daughter and ex-wife in adolescence, lissome and pre-mascaraed.

"Be nice. There's no need for anyone blowing up at anybody this early in—"

"You're the one who's blowing up! You're blowing up all over the freaking internet, not to mention my whole li—"

"Can you please just come sit down and eat breakfast before—"

"I am coming!"

Exit stage left, followed by cloud of abrasive perfume designed to cover periodsmell, in a huff of secret murmurings and whispers.

"But you're not even breathing heavy."

He flipped over the slab of toast after prying its burnt side free with the spatula, trading vestal white for black. *Bite off my left ear, add cannibalizing to yo charges. Sheeet. I got me this pastyass white boy getting fucked up on the backside. They fucking him up real good.* "Jesus Christ," sighed Dagonet to no one, including himself. *What? You think I ain't no real French toast? I's the Frenchest toast they is. Polly-vous Franzia, motherfucker? I say Frenchtalk like: Grand Marnier. Chambord. Courvoisier, motherfucker. Been born and raised in the hood up in Cannes. That's why they call me a convict, get it? Sheeet. They frying us up real good. The governor, he eat me alive fore banging the maid.* He didn't think he was probably going to prison; he was merely going to be shunned by all and sundry, a pariah from all acclaim, fame, all major top-tier awards. The only Oscar he'd ever hold would be Mayer. They were taking his adoring fans—a few diehards would assuredly stick with him—but worse, he'd forever be branded a pervert. He'd been a pervert, but now he really was one.

Now no one will watch me. Yes, as in jack off with my penis. What do you think I meant? Practice my tai chi? Fuck you. I've got news for all of you: I got all you guys' consents to be a complete and shameless pervert when you paid me three hundred greenbacks for galleryfuckingseating, so fuck it; I'll reach climax right here in front of you, and I dare you to sue me. I'll fight this to the Supreme Court. The whole courtroom'll be covered in unconsensual semen. Mine and Brett Kavanaugh's. Now where was I . . .

The phone rang. It was Dyson.

"Crisis hotline. Press one to speak to Our Savior. Two to be arsed by Judge Kavanaugh. Three for methampheta—"

"Okay, let me dictate the terms under which I might not maybe be quitting. One: as much as I feel the sting of putting my foot down on this, you agree to cancel your shows for at least the coming month. It could be longer, a lot longer; we'll have to wait and measure the fallout. Oh, and whatever you do stay away from the frigging turncoat media. This Fischer twat who ran the article was practically handed his career on a silver platter when I granted him an interview with Jim Carrey. I phoned him up this morning; I said, 'Don't tell me you don't identify? As one male to another.' And do you know what that prick said? Smug son of a bitch, he goes, 'Sure I identify. What guy wouldn't? It's just that I got mouths to feed, and try explaining that to Gene, that he can't feed them with only his dick out.' Can you believe the balls of that cocksucker? Right, where was I? Point number two: you agree to do a cameo of repentance on, oh, I don't know, say something like *The View*, which would be a godsend, in which case we get the high priestess Barbara Walters to absolve you before God and country for your wayward ways. And three, and most important: you agree to having this op-ed piece, a rebuttal of sorts and confession, a concession to the hysterical Cult of Death, I had my new intern write published in the *Times*, in which you come clean to having been molested as an altar boy—we won't name names, but seeing as you're from Boston, anyone's guess is good as to the antecedent—and you admit to undergoing therapy for years to curb your problem."

"My problem? *Mais mon problème, c'est quoi?*"

"That you are sexually attracted to women and fail not to act upon it after not receiving consent."

"But I did receive it, Dyson! That's the whole thing! I said, 'Do you awfully mind if I forthwith refresh my dick with some gusto?' to which the gentlelady then responded—"

"Don't say that! For the love of God, please don't fucking say that. Just roll over and admit to everything. I don't care; even if you actually didn't do it, which I'm pretty certain you probably did, admit to everything this bitch is saying and play up the card you've been molested. That's the only way out of this. Just think of poor Paul Reubens. There: I just sent you the file."

"Muhct muh juhstk Fchtuht uhmuhmff."

"You're telling me you can't read with French toast in your fat fucking belchend?"

There was batter and butter all over his fingers. Most pornstars after a gangbang were cleaner.

"Hey, tell your intern I said thanks for having me molested again, but I really sincerely believe once this whole thing blows over a comeback—"

"Why you egotistical exhibitionist! There is no comeback tour if your head is stuck on a pike and they parade it up Fifth Avenue for these raging tribades—I'm sorry, forgive me, for these people experiencing periods—and there will sure as shit be no comeback if you don't have a manager to sweep things under the rug. Now you will agree to having this published—that or you can kiss your famous fat ass goodbye."

"Yeah, sorry," said Dagonet, eager to get off the phone. His younger daughter of five, Erica, had just sashayed in, still wearing pajamas. "Hey, I've got to go, old buddy. I've got my nuts to scratch." And hung up the phone.

"Daddy, is there breakfast?"

"There is breakfast, peanut. Why aren't you getting ready for school?"

At which moment he realized he'd been eating all the French toast. In waiting for his progeny to manifest, he'd gone on eating. The child was scratching her genitals.

"Don't do that, kitten."

The revelation of the refrigerator's bowels told him there were no more eggs with which to render the batter by which to contrive French toast.

"Why?"

"Because it's not polite. Sit at the table." She bounded toward her chair.

Ever since he'd been a teenager the real meaning of his existence had been a trial of one misadventure after the next, as if the world had been created and designed specifically for the purpose of giving him every opportunity for failure. Of course with women and getting laid, but even with his family and his own dog he had never made solid contact. The rest of them seemed to be going through life rather painless, and their watching him have to suffer, he could sense, made them uncomfortable. It wasn't until later, until college, that he started to count it a gain to be scrutinized from without by people who utterly hated him and who propelled his failures: with comedy he could at least keep them coming back. And yet somewhere in there things had gotten quite muddled, all turned around. Perhaps the whole ordeal was a blessing, the universe's way of nudging him to spend more time at home with his family. He would buy them a house in the Catskills, where they'd learn the names of constellations and build a fire, say, by rubbing two sticks together. Like gay guys getting it on.

"Here, have some cereal."

"I WANT FRENCH TOAST!"

"It's just like French toast, sweetheart. It's sugary and moist and nutritionally defective. Why aren't you sitting?"

"Because . . . it feels weird."

She was standing, tugging at the crotch of her pants.

"Did you do something to your tutu?"

Her failure to affirm him was an affirmation in itself.

"Rats, not another marble!"

Thus, after washing his hands of batter, after extracting the marble from the dwarf female's hymen as he ran through the multiplication tables (his dick, at times, requested that he be permitted to lend his two cents, but the master directed he be kept at bay), after washing his befouled hands once more and restraining himself from asking, "Was it good?" then after another two shots of Rémy thrown back in the bedroom, they were sitting around the table.

"FIVE-MINUTE WARNING! I REALLY MEAN IT THIS TIME!"

The reindeer jingle of anarchy pants juxtaposed with the heavy-soled pedal point of Doc Martens presaged his elder daughter or vampire version sucked dry by various childhood traumas of his fashioning and neglect.

"I thought we're having French toast?" said the chinadoll. She looked strangely younger, this ghost of Christmases past three sheets to the wind.

"Plans have changed. We're having cereal."

"I don't want cereal," said that black slash mouth. To cover the mottling of the scars she was wearing an assembly of studded leather bracelets, light BDSM gear. Well suited, conceived as she was in whips and chains.

"You have leave to choose not to eat cereal."

"Then why were you making French toast?"

She had him by the scrotum, just like her mother.

"Turns out the bread was moldy."

"Liar, you ate it all. I'm going back to my room. Call me when we're really leaving. Try not rape anybody in the meantime."

"We're leaving right now!" proclaimed Dagonet. "And I did not, DID NOT RAPE ANYBODY!"

As he resumed slurping sugary milk from a plastic spoon, somewhere in that storm-surged sewer of a conscience he wondered what had ever spurred him to be so presumptuous as to think he could improve on his parents' doing. As if simply because he were he he could do much better. Family: a cesspool you take turns filling until all of you drown or expire in the act.

"What's rape?" inquired the child, goateed with the lactate of cows.

"It's nothing, princess," said Dagonet, watching himself speak. He felt the phone ringing. It was Jane. "Shit."

"Is rape an ape?"

He motioned her to hush like you'd fan out a naughty fire.

"You Jane, me Tarzan!"

"Jesus Christ, I can't believe this is happening," said the voice. "I assumed divorce would solve eighty-three percent of our problems, but I literally cannot get away from you everywhere I turn. Tell me it isn't true. It's all over the news. Did you really do what she claims?"

"Probably," said Dagonet, too lamely.

"Jesus Christ, the children."

"Rape is an ape is a grape is a tape is a lape . . ."

Motioning, shooing her. Then getting up and sprinting for the solitude of the shitter.

"What's she saying?"

"I have no idea," said Dagonet. While he ran, ensuring the screening of his junk. "However, I'm beginning to wonder whether you may have dropped her on something unbendy."

He shut the door, locked it. Immediately the cramped sterile space smelling sweetly of feminine hygiene ensconced him in something akin to relief. The toilet gaped at him unflushed. Who'da thunk the little cunt had so much pee in her? Then as a deflective balestra: "We had another marble incident this morning."

Sigh: storm surge of the weeping woman.

"What did you guys do?"

"What did we do? Oh, well, we played ten rounds of Chinese checkers with our lingam and dingam, followed by a long discussion on the anagogical benefits of *My Little Pony*. What do you think we did? Daddy rolled up his sleeves and dove for a pearl in his little girl's oyster. It was traumatic mostly for one of us. I'm gonna need a serious shrink with superpsychic abilities to prescribe me the waters of Lethe."

"Dr. Coffin said she learned it from some boy in school, but I'm beginning to wonder if it isn't an indication of something else. Something much worse. Do you think it could be one of the teachers? They say there should always be two of them there in the room, but the janitors, you know, they get to come and go at large out of the bathrooms however they please. Has she mentioned anything to you along those lines?"

"It's probably, you know, kids just being kids. Totally normal stuff."

"Ugh," her voice was sitting up in her bosom. "Ugh" was the motto of the terrible Cult of Death with two beavers rampant, which one faithfully translated as "All Men Must Die." "You of all people have no basis to judge normality, Gene, not for children, nor for adults. Every year you get ten times worse. Fatter and more a sloven, digging deeper into your most outrageous instincts. And now this. Our marriage was always a mockery, but this simply confirms it. I knew back then you were doing things behind my back, and one day it will be unavoidable for them to know too, for them to see what kind of monster you enjoy touting, but this goes beyond anything like the dictates of art. This stigma, they'll have to live with it their whole lives."

He looked out the window, onto 10th and 23rd. Already tourists were crowding the High Line. Far below a homeless man was leaning against the door of, pissing on the boarded-up Half King. If he craned his too sullied neck, in the distance he could barely make out a sliver of the Hudson flowing to the Atlantic, to some other country.

"Look, I . . . I didn't mean . . . I guess I always thought the money and fame would shield them from all the craziness, but now I'm realizing it only exposed them to more . . . and by 'them' I mean the goth dyke and the slut with the very improper marble trick."

Consent. Let me tell all you fellows: there's only one night you ever truly receive her consent, and that's the night you pop the question. That's the only night where you can do anything on the planet, no questions asked. But for a man it's totally wasted. It's like eating a big piece of birthday cake while you're on your way to the electric chair. *Who wants a delicious helping of birthday cake when you're thirty seconds from dead?*

"So I'm calling the lawyer, and I'll be asking her about going to court. I think sharing custody is a horrible mistake. They should know your environment is toxic. They'll know that already, I'm afraid."

Last time he was in court he signed a DVD, hoping it would ingratiate him to the judge, whom he twice made chuckle in his defense, the whole ordeal leaving him feeling prostitutey and smutty.

"Just answer one question: How can a forty-six-year-old man still know nothing whatsoever about life? What is your big secret?"

The bathtub was still full of bathwater. Alexandra had forgotten to unstopper the drain. On the window ledge lay the hair dryer. Dagonet plugged it in, the appliance a child's spacegun. He entered the tub, underclothes and everything, holding on to the phone, the wet water smelling soapy, barely lukewarm, feeling like some place he was supposed to be, and lowered himself down to the chin, head afloat and rubenesque paunch.

Dear world, I apologize. My go-to hangup: How can I be so selfish while being so damn selfless?

"That I know life's secret," said Dagonet in his voice of honest sincerity.

"What's that, Gene?"

"The secret to life is it's a dirty little secret."

At quarter to eleven the first exiters, a well-dressed couple swinging hands, came out, buoyant and laughing, as they raced to grab the first cab. Within the minute others had followed, and then the rest of the cabs that had been lingering by the Beacon were gone, and then it was a race as to who could be farthest up Broadway to hail a cab before everyone else.

They were still coming out and thronging the curb like they were waiting for a parade when Lance came up to the table.

"You've been here this whole time?" He took off his jacket, hung it over the chair, sat, and rolled up his sleeves.

"How was it?" said Margaret.

The waiter came over and took his drink order.

"Okay," he said, extending himself once the waiter had gone.

"Was there a full house?"

"The house was pretty full," said Lance after some thought, "but the applause wasn't as strong as you'd think."

She stopped what she was doing and closed the computer and swept the machine aside. She looked at the man to scrutinize him. How she regarded him implied she held the power to determine whether or not he was lying. Apart from a vase with a single red rose and the menu erect behind it, the only items on the table were her laptop and a cup of coffee.

"Did he mention me at all? Did he say what a shameless, selfish prick he is?"

"To the latter matter: yes. At least a dozen times. Likely several. But so far as the former question: not really. The cue ball said nothing whatsoever about the incident. The ribald baldy."

She spat, a quick blast of air, not quite a sigh, not quite a laugh. What else to say but had you heard the sound from some dentist's apparatus it would make perfect sense?

"That's all you're going to say?"

The waiter came over and put the gin martini down on a napkin.

"What else do you want me to say?"

"How about, for one thing, was he funny?"

The man sipped his martini. He liked playing the game with himself of guessing the type of gin they used in restaurants. Tanqueray, he guessed. Nothing swanky. He picked up the menu, skimmed it. It said the house gin was Beefeater.

"Was he funny?" the man at last repeated. "I'd be lying if I said nobody laughed. But, you know, they were probably his cult of diehard fans, come to send him off with their goodwill. The turnout of the next shows, you know, once he starts heading south, away from his base, will likely be pretty dismal. Plenty of boos from plenty of protesters."

"But tonight: Was he funny?"

He watched her surveying his expression. Things wanting to burgeon from his brain, wrong little seeds waiting to flower to thought.

"Isn't that his job?"

"Did you ever laugh?"

"Did I ever laugh?" The question itself made him chuckle. The man was her twin brother.

With both hands he held and sipped the martini. If they were still here when he finished, he'd ask the waiter about ordering another with Tanqueray, just to be clear of the difference.

"Once," said Lance. "Just once. Laughed as in out loud."

"And what exactly did you find so funny?" She was watching him the way she had whenever he had stolen into her room and done something he was not supposed to and had no way of answering or defending himself, only to have gone back in time and not done it, she who had been more of a mother to him than his own, lady and lord alike. He scanned the martini, as if in looking he might imbibe.

"The closest he got to mentioning the whole incident . . . well, let me go backward. When he came out he said he was no longer to be referred to anymore as Dagonet, but from now on his new name was Tummytuck."

"Tummytuck?"

"Yeah, Tummytuck."

"As in he had one?"

"I don't know. Maybe. Yeah maybe, probably, sure. He did look pretty fit now that I come to think of it. For once he was wearing a suit, and he was even pretty cleanshaven. But let's see, the only time I ever recall really laughing—and laughing as in hysterical—was when he pulled down his pants—"

"He pulled down his pants?"

"—was when he pulled down his pants before the audience and showed us he no longer had any . . . any . . . ding-a-ling." The man's lips were folded over his teeth, his eyes small. "He . . . he said, 'You can tell who's no longer *dictating* things.' He . . ." He could no longer talk, just bite the inside of his cheek.

"Are you saying he had himself castrated?"

Subsequent to clearing his throat, "I really don't honestly know," said Lance with an oversized frown, "but whatever he did, it was pretty hysterical."

Margaret removed her eyes from the man and rubbed her hands.

"Sure, okay. I'll show you something."

She took her computer, which she had brushed off to the side, unfolded it, and instantly the light from the screen illuminated her gaze. Within it there stirred a vitality that was claiming the eagerness of her face into something of a smile. Her brother snorted, reached for a sip of his drink. This calmed him down.

"You've been working on jokes of your own, have you?"

"No," she batted this away. "Read." Turning to him the light of the computer.

"I can't. You read. I can't see good in the dark."

"I spent the last half hour crafting this to the op-ed editor of the *Times*. It's only a taste of what's still to come. Tell me what do you think: *Dear Editor, With the commencement of Gene Dagonet's 'A Wang Is a Wong Is a Dong: Unrepentant World Mystery Tour,' the writing is clear on the marquee. Does the title alone not signify his intent is purely profane? How can a body of discerning critics and audiences not only grant him their easy forgiveness, and for acts for which he has so stolidly refused to claim ownership, but even more confoundingly, offer money at his cloven feet? As has been intimated these last months, there are several others of us who have experienced violations and transgressions—repeated acts of serious harm—at the instigation of this predator, many of whom will soon be coming forward with stories far worse than my own. In the meantime let it suffice those comedy-loving members of the public who have any self-respect and purport a reasonable love for the art to understand that indifference is the purest form of retaliation to Mr. Dagonet's upcoming tour and that they should rally their efforts to prevent making his comeback a victory. Signed, Margaret King.* So: What do you think?"

The brother, tilting the glass of the martini and waiting for the gin to invade his lips, realized there was nothing more left to drink.

"That's good. It ought to hit him right where it hurts. Once they come forward, do you think then you'll end—"

"End?" she cut the man off. What prompted her laughter was glee. "Why this is only the beginning!"

Evil in the Object

FOR A WHILE I thought love meant the same thing as doing something somebody else wanted. Meant making someone happy. Even if what they wanted might have been wrong. Love was beyond everything.

My parents told me if I ever moved to the city, they'd never come visit me, which was reason enough to move.

He'd been working as a cook. Everyone knew him as undependable. They'd give him orders, and maybe he'd make their food. They hated getting stuck explaining to customers why they'd been waiting an hour for their omelet.

When the boss told him he was through, he took off his apron and laid it down as if he'd been expecting it. Real calm. The boss waving everywhere and hooting and hollering like he was the one in trouble. Elrod just walked over, the two of them matched to the elbows, his hairnet and apron burning in the kitchen, and punched him in the mouth. He fought the whole lot of them until he heard sirens. Then he made a break for the door.

Later he was there in the parking lot, giving himself a haircut in the mirror on his bike.

"Good for you," he said.

"What?"

The sheers he was using, I'd seen them somewhere—he'd hawked them from the things in the kitchen.

"I said, 'Good for you.' Good for you for dumping those blackberry pancakes all over the geriatric brigade at table ten. You tell them to go stuff it?"

"It was an accident. He said I reminded them of their granddaughter. Mr. Heffner comped their breakfast."

Elrod laughed.

"Oh, that's rich," he said. "I'm sure old Heffy's tickled to death. Are you fired?"

"He let me off with a warning."

"Why don't you just go on in there and quit."

Elrod was good to me. He saw my true potential. He saw me for what I was. No one before had ever perfectly identified my faults. And didn't care.

Growing up, he'd been a Mormon. I never knew there was such thing before as Mormons in Canada, but I guess if I'd thought about it, I'd probably have thought there was.

"Dear lord," said Bermet.

"What?"

Pointing at my hip, at a patch of bare skin.

"He beating on you?"

"Oh."

"Is he beating on you?"

The bell dinged, and the new cook, a friend of Elrod, put up the order for table four.

"Come back here."

When I came back she pulled up my shirt.

"I know a shelter for battered women," she said, studying the color. "Does that hurt?"

"I'm not battered."

"I'd say you aren't."

"I'm not being battered."

"Not for no pancakes." She pulled up further my shirt. "Honey, you need to run."

"It's not like that."

"I'd say it isn't."

Her fingers felt dry and cold.

"You know you don't have to take it. You're better than that."

I twisted, recovering my shirt. The bell dinged again.

"It's not like that. It's just that . . . he likes it . . ." As I passed by she lifted an eyebrow. "Rough."

When I came back her arms were folded, her legs in a stance, and she was seriously smacking her gum.

"Honey, the real question is: Do you?"

I liked the times we listened to music. We'd be sitting, or on his bed. It'd be something his band would play, or would be thinking about playing. The room all covered in noise. And the two of us feeling the same feeling. It didn't even have to be good. I just liked that he was there, feeling the same way.

On a weekend in November they had a gig down in Corpus Christi. It just happened to be my day off. One of his friends knew someone who had a house, where the two of us were invited to stay.

That next morning we went on the beach. The surf was rough and the sand was frozen. We didn't care. The sea smelled old and full of authority, though I'd forgotten to bring our swimsuits.

For a while we sat on the pier and watched the waves come in. They'd try to make their way to the shore. But they'd just break into other waves or join with others. The ones that finally did, only tiny bits ever reached the sand.

"What in the malebolge was that?"
"Ow. Ow!"
"What, did you burn yourself?"
He listened while I told him how I'd fell and hit my cheek on the grill. He laughed.
"What, did you slip on a banana peel?"

The whole ride home Elrod was sullen. My cheek felt like it had melted, but whenever I went to touch it, the skin was still there, only tender. It didn't matter. Something inside me had come alive.
On coming into the city, we saw that stepladder pyramid sidestep into view.
Then at home he was yelling. Calling me psycho. Calling me crazy. He said I needed real mental help. That I'd *enjoyed* burning myself on the oven. Had done it on purpose. He knew, because he was like me too. Only he'd tried to snap me out of it. To show me the pain was only a means, a necessary hurdle for becoming stronger, that there was a way of harnessing it, not an absolute end in itself. He said this was the same with love. I said I agreed.

A whirlpool of people. Half nude and glistening like fish trying to jump back to the water. The whole room circling, wheel over wheel, and before I know the draw of the current pulls me to its vortex, to become part of the spinning—flipping and glistening, helping each other when we fall—the crowd pushing into us as they try to keep from being pulled in while Elrod's music crowds taste-sighthearingsense. Elrod perched above on the stage. Watching us spinning. Proud it's to his liking. Everything is a whirlpool, and I am covered hair to ankle with those stickers that say the name of Elrod's band, and everyone is laughing. Glad because we're wrong.

The person who I am is dangling from the ceiling, a flag for reviling, prey in the hands of claws, no identity but the missiles of spit they send through the great swaddling of doomful noise. The room awash in screams. Somewhere among them is Elrod.

For a while we'd been at each other's throats. There were worries about money, about what to eat. About who did what. The place had become a pigsty.

 I'd been on him for a while about hanging a blinder to cover the window. It could've been there for weeks. I figured it was just something he'd got, something that had fallen in his way. But for whatever reason it bothered me.

Sometimes I spent hours gazing and staring up at it. Tried to extract it so that there were just shapes and colors, staring at it until it was something it no longer was—some colorful kind of sign—but whenever I moved close, I saw the blood in that sea of red suddenly spilling over everything, in that geometry of stars in a cross, at first just the pattern of figured-out lines, the stars of a lynch mob gathering for some person to be hanged.

Eventually I took it down and threw it in the recycling. That he would notice was doubtful. And if he did would hardly care.

But a few days later he'd bought a decal and put it right over the center of his bike where everyone could see what he thought. Even if he didn't, as only I knew. Still, the thing itself really bothered me. Began bothering me more and more. Would creep into my unexpected thoughts. For how many hours I spent thinking on it—who could say. The image of its being itched at me like a sore, and I managed to scratch off part of it, but not without scratching off some of the finish.

That's when we had it out.

"How come you care so much about the Confederate flag? You're not even from the South."

"It's not that I care," he said. "I find it interesting."

"How?"

"It's a reminder about history."

"Yeah, but for all the wrong reasons."

"Okay."

"Don't you know what it represents?"

"I'm not about all that," said Elrod. "I just dig the way it looks. And if you're intent on twisting my nuts, then you can voetsek with the rest of them."

On a weekday in February he left without coming back. When a few days passed, I assumed he must have left on tour. If he had told me, I didn't remember. Things were close to pretty desperate. I'd quit my job a while back, and there was no money in the house, and the lights had been turned off. I ate some crackers his roommate had left on the counter.

He came back with his beard in a braid and looking pleased with himself because he'd gotten two things. There had been plenty of time for me to hate him, and now that I saw him again in the flesh, I realized how I'd hated him all along. Even when we'd been happy. He was looking pleased with himself on account of two things: The Reviled had gotten a record deal, a small label, but a label nonetheless, and were supposed to start recording, and he had also got a tattoo. He wore fishnet so everyone could see. A great Confederate flag slapped across the knot of his chest. Waving between the nipples.

"Do you like it?" he said.

I knew he'd done it to irk me. To get underneath my skin. To show me I didn't matter. A while ago I'd made up my mind to leave him, and now that it was decided, I knew I could use it to show him he meant nothing to me as well. I'd been acting all over again to please him, and where had that led me but in neither party being happy but only wanting—wanting more and more. If Elrod from the get-go had duped me, I was the one more wrong for letting myself be duped.

"Do you like it?" I said.

"Like? Ha! Even *hate* is too light a word. If I could efface it into oblivion, I still wouldn't be content. Not until all living memory of everything that depended on you and your dykey haircut was rendered nada, nil."

When we went out that night, he kept referring to me as "the monk" or "Butch Cassidy." I think he wanted to take me out as bait to lure girls. To see if I was attractive. A few started coming close, but as soon as he swooped between us, they took off. They sensed he was expecting to get laid.

At one point Elrod went off and left. I could see him by the bar, these guys pointing to his chest, flapping their jackets, but I didn't care. Not even when they led him outside. I was dancing and not thinking about anyone and what they wanted, only myself. Dancing and feeling good.

He was there, curled up in the parking lot like a run-over eagle, bloody and mostly unconscious, when we walked out.

"Isn't that the guy you came in with?" She would have pointed, but her hand threw both of ours in front.

"That's nobody."

The Elegance of Simplicity

"Let me tell you a story about why I'm telling you a story," says Andy.

After an instructive semester abroad, I'd come to the conclusion that shouldn't surprise anybody that the Brits have one of three types of faces: a porridge face, a pudding face, or a haggis face, into the latter of which type falls Andy.

Tonight, however, on his one night in town, he shows up at the hotel bar with a huge patch of gauze over the left cheek of his haggis face, likely the souvenir of his hurting himself when drunk, or perhaps Babs slapped him around, or perhaps he was tickling his cat—who knows—but the point of this souvenir of whatever incident is that it's served as another excuse for Andy to go on one of his pet subjects, his railing against the American health-care system and its host of wild incompetents, apparently who have led to his being triaged in a manner he doesn't see fit, and Bernie-Sanders this, and we-should-all-go-be-like-Denmark that . . . since every other year or so Andy and Babs come over to carouse and tour the old plantations.

"A few hours earlier. As regards me, Babs, a mutual friend of ours by the name of Johnnie Walker, and a chavvy and highly pugnacious albeeno who, judging by the likes of his dress and character, was in all probability Kentish."

He tells me how he and Babs were out drinking in the Quarter and were accosted by a girl who invited them back for a drink. As she's closing up the bar, a ruckus ensues from the corner, in the midst of which there is an albeeno hollering at the pitch of his lungs: "Kill all the gays!"

"You can't say that!" yells the girl and tells them it's time to go. Which they do, except for the albeeno, who, it turns out, is the girl's boyfriend.

So as they're going for the house, the whole way there the albeeno is staggering, stopping strangers, and interrogating them as to whether or not they prefer copulating with partners of the same sex, going on about bad blood and how the solution to curing AIDS is simple: got to kill all the gay people.

Once they're at the house, she tucks the albeeno abed, but as Andy and Babs are waiting for the girl to emerge from the hall, they hear a ruckus commence from the bedroom, where they run back to find the albeeno wailing on the poor bartender. Andy lunges over, in the midst of which struggle the albeeno bites him good on the knuckles—Andy shows me the lunettes over his knuckles, which freshly ooze as he clenches his fist—a crazy glint in those pale eyes—around which time he knocks him out cold. "Sod it!" says the girl-bartender. "He's been doing this all week, my albeeno."

But that's not the end.

On their way back to the hotel—Andy at this point is dabbing his knuckles with the paper of some receipt—they're waylaid by a mugger. "Youse! Don't turn your backs on me!" "Oh, shut your dobber! What's it your hankering?" says Andy, finally had it with the man's heckling. "Very well," says the punk, "your wallet!" "It's yours," says Andy, "if you fancy to take it." At which point Andy engages in his second contest of strength for the evening, and the two men are on the ground, tumbling over the cobblestones, while

Babs is looking on, tired of Andy's nonsense. "Can you give him your wallet and quit your fooling?" Eventually Andy runs the guy off, but not before he's scratched good on the cheek—hence the huge patch of gauze—and next thing they know they're on their way to the hospital to get Andy stitches.

"AIDS blood," says Andy. "That chavvy albeeno, he was hollering on about AIDS, about hating the gays and all, and I'm sitting there, having a think on it: Why else to hate homosexuals unless there's something they done in the first place? As in all this hooting and hollering is an airing of grievances for infecting him with AIDS?"

"You mean you think the fellow had AIDS?"

"Aye," says Andy, "it's not entirely impossible. Anyways, I was getting to thinking there in that hospital: Which means if that albeeno fellow had AIDS, and there was a drawing of mutual bloods, it means that I have AIDS as well. But," he takes a sip of his pint, downs most of his pint, his third—I think he must relax his gag reflex whenever he drinks, something I've always been meaning to ask him about—and now his face beams down, "it therefore follows I gave the mugger my AIDS as well!"

Andy jostles me in the ribs, and a few patrons crane their necks or turn their heads on account of how loudly Andy bellows. But no one seems upset, since who wouldn't want a big burly Scot laughing at the top of his lungs in the hotel bar? Whenever Andy and Babs come to town, which is rarer these days ever since their son Walter Scott withdrew from Tulane, this is where they stay: the renovated Capitol Center, with its historic portraits and expensive still lifes and perfume of fresh wallpaper, which for the longest time was the derelict Heidelberg, where people only went to do meth and transients retired to die. "But they wouldn't test me for no AIDS, your fangle of a health-care bureaucracy. Got to wait for the old NHS." He sighs, not without scorn. "Hey," he only now notices my rocks glass is full of sparkling water, "what have we there, fizzy juice? On the wagon are we?"

"I gotta be at work in an hour," I go. "If they smell booze on my breath, they'll fire me on the spot."

"Cock a snook at them," says Andy. He signals the bartender to bring him his fourth pint. "You should transfer your trade to Scotland. If you're not a wee bit hoolit whilst on the clock, you're not doing your job." Andy laughs, and I laugh too, but my laughter isn't real. Now that I stop to think about it, I can feel everyone's faces on me, paused in the midst of their meals, staring at us, motionless and judging, judging with their thoughtlessness. What precisely they want they cannot come out and say, but I know what they are trying to say in spite of themselves: They say our universe is a bubble among bubbles, among a whole bushel of bubbles infinite, and it is on days like this that I keep waiting for one of those other bubbles to come colliding against ours, and before you know it . . . POP!

Andy is tall, and I am standing almost up under his chin, in the frame of his lank black greasy hair, so that whenever he speaks, I can feel his baritone come booming through my sternum. His voice is powerful; it is a voice neither good nor bad. Including the matter of what he is saying. Not that it leaves me indifferent, but then none of it rouses me to passion. I am just letting his voice wash over me like a neutral bath. The only real clue I can guess as to how I'm supposed to be feeling about sharing this moment with Andy is that I am waiting somehow, not waiting for my chance to talk so much as for these people at their tables and in their chairs and on their barstools to burst of a sudden like bubbles.

"While we're on the subject of scars, you got any fresh ones you care to body forth? Any compliments of the job, wrangling rascals to the ground or behind bars? Saving the planet from pernicious filth?"

My job as a campus night watchman never ceases to fascinate Andy, who prefers to imagine it in a romantic strain of something like an episode of *Dragnet* or *Law & Order*, with me fighting crime and keeping the city a little bit safer at night—which is not how it works at all.

"Oh, just a few scuffles with drunks, in which case we call the cops to come put the cuffs on. Nothing crazy. A few suicides every year during finals. Car thieves, vandals. Nothing glamorous."

"Right, there's your problem. People are too bloody nice in this neck of the country. Or at least they're good at pretending to be, which is roughly equivalent to the same thing. Which might make them all the more susceptible, I'd say, to being in trouble. Let's order you more of that fizzy water." He signals to the bartender while retrieving his fresh pint. "But don't go crazy. This isn't a race."

"I wish I had some stories. But I tell you what, when faced with fourteen dollars an hour and Kaiser Permanente, I stick with the elegance of simplicity."

"The elegance of simplicity?"

"Exactly." Andy's bandaged haggis face blinks down, as if wondering indeed what's not to stop us from splintering into particles in an incredible cosmic explosion. "For instance, let's say there's a gun on the floor by someone's head—not that this has ever happened—but let's say for the sake of the scenario. I don't misdoubt for a second it's a suicide. Fourteen dollars an hour gets you the elegance of simplicity. No drug lord planted the weapon, no ex-wife seeking revenge. If the suspect hasn't turned right, then, according to the elegance of simplicity, one correctly thereupon deduces that the suspect must have turned . . ."

"Left?"

"You're getting it. And if the apple hasn't gone up, then chances are it must have gone—"

"Down."

"You're a natural."

"Braw, I'm a simple kind of guy."

"Honestly the last scar I remember was—"

"Arthur's Seat," says Andy. There is a sacredness to his voice.

"Yeah, up there on Arthur's Seat."

What Andy is referring to is, after meeting twenty years ago at the Sandy Bells bar at a ceilidh, where he kept a bee on a string of floss and would thrust a black and white old-timey photograph of people getting it on into the faces of perfect strangers, the event that continues to bring us together.

"Are you a lover or are you a fighter?" proposed Andy, the bee buzzing between us and me swatting it out of my frown. I'd never met him before until that second.

"I'm just a guy drinking a beer."

"Good lad!" said Andy, and pretty soon we had hit it off, though not without him periodically interrupting in order to ask some perplexed stranger if he or she identified more as a lover or more as a fighter. Finally some old tosser at the bar goes, "Neither! I'm both!" That about blew the lid off Andy's top. "Both?" he shouted. "Both!" It was like Newton alighting on gravity. "If that's not the dream, what is? This calls for an occasion!" Upon which statement I followed Andy and his bee up to the summit of Arthur's Seat, guided only by Andy's determination and the moonlight and lights of the city, upon which we swore a blood oath ever to remain a lover as well as a fighter. With my souvenir for a scar across my palm, I thought I was pretty slick, coming home from being abroad, but my mother soon made it plain she disapproved of my new worldly swagger. Now the scar is hardly perceivable, looks more like a weird ridge upsetting the web of my palm, and as I look at that shape from long ago, a symbol, it seems, of youth and its blind optimism rendered another old wound, I steal a glance at my watch. Almost time to hurry home, then head to work. And yet what's to stop me from following Andy, apart from the logistical headache of moving across the Atlantic?

"Say, you remember that little hen you fell head over heels in love for?" says Andy. "The one you printed all those papers you were planning to tape over town? You remember? 'God's angel,' you declared, no less."

How could I forget. One spring morning I canceled a trip leaving Haymarket after catching eyes with the most beautiful fruition of the cosmos, for she was living proof that the working definition of *beauty* was nothing less than a catastrophe. We stared at each other across the platform. "Hi," I mouthed. "Hi," she mouthed back. It was obvious we loved each other straightaway. Then came her train. It was only then I realized we weren't so star-crossed as the train tracks between us had led me to believe, so I raced around to her side, only to find the doors of the train had closed, her eyes resting on me a final, ethereal instant as the train accelerated away. So I did what would any lovestruck dolt would do: I made three hundred flyers that read:

Missed connection

You were staring at me

You caught the 9:30 south at Haymarket

Call me

And included a number.

With my stack of three hundred flyers and roll of heavy-duty tape, I'd run into Andy as I was leaving the copiers.

"In love are we?" he said on inspecting my note.

"Andy, *love* is too weak a word."

Before going back to the station, where I'd tape all the papers, we went to a chippy on Broughton, and who should walk right out of the door as we were going in but the red-haired girl, the angel, God's gift!

"That was her!"

"No way! You can't be serious. Miss Universe? Well, what are you waiting for? Now is the big occasion, before she gets sucked away in the mystery of time."

"Yeah, but," I said there sorrowfully, trying to fit it correctly to words, "she wasn't as pretty up close as she was from far away."

And that was the end of that.

"I wonder what she's doing at this very moment," muses Andy. Most of the new pint is gone.

"The elegance of simplicity would deduce she is married and has a few kids."

"Does the elegance of simplicity account for whether or not she has retained her beauty?"

"The elegance of simplicity would wager she is now in her late thirties and that, while pretty, her looks are running out. The elegance of simplicity does not look favorably upon women over forty. Apart from Babs, of course. Babs is a Pictish princess."

Andy's dark haggis face wrinkles and simpers, biting that sausage protrusion of a tongue; he clinks my glass. He admires my calculated phrasing as I admire his volubility.

"I'll pass along your regards."

In truth, Babs has never been very beautiful, has always been one of those solid Scottish women who are built for long sunless winters and Nordic winds, with their layer of blubber and their squat, solid figure, like the compact embodiment of Presbyterianism itself. These days, whenever they come to town, she stays in the hotel while Andy and I go out. She and Becky Jo used to get along pretty well. Whenever they'd pass through town, they usually came to the house, and the four of us would stay up through the night talking and laughing. Then it got to be where people, not only Babs and Andy . . . you could tell they were pretending, or rather, you could tell they were pretending to ignore him, lying there on the couch. And if that doesn't kill a conversation, I don't know what will. I guess Babs figures, and figures correctly, that I need these intense one on ones of Andy's male company, and she is probably grateful for the hour of peace in the hotel.

"Tell her I say hello."

"Of course. She wants you for a visit. You can stay as long as you like. We'll lend you the keys; you'll come and go as you please. Take you to Skye, over to Orkney. To plenty of picture-perfect postcard places."

"That's what I don't understand. You have plenty of pretty old houses in your country. What's the big deal about ours?"

"Well, we did have plenty of pretty old houses; we did now, but, you see, we tore them all down in our brawls. At least in your wars youse had the keen sense of foresight to allow some of them to remain upstanding."

I look at my watch.

"I'm really sorry, but I need to jet."

"Right, no bother. Babs and I have an early departure ourselves." Andy braces himself around the anchor of his glass, his black eyes sloshing. "But you haven't yet said how's the little one. Doing okay?"

"He's not so little anymore. In fact he's exactly the same."

"Is that so good?"

"Good would be him going to football games and getting speeding tickets and chasing skirts and having his heart broken—

but, no, he's right there on the couch where you last left him, same place, lying down."

I can tell that Andy regrets raising the subject, knew he would regret raising it, but felt compelled to in spite of any fleeting discomfort, like giving grandma, with all her dentures and whiskers, a smooch on the lips.

"Isn't there some kind of place, you know, that would offer to take him? Take him for a while off your hands. Take good care of him."

"Like what kind of place?" I say as I set down my sparkling water and button my coat, signs I must, if don't want to, go.

"A place for . . ."

"For people who have only brain stems? Sure, let me know when you find one of those. No, I'm sorry. I didn't mean to be standoffish."

"I just want you to be happy, Wils. That's my number-one priority. Yours, my own, and Babs."

"Thanks, but I am happy," I say, aware that these days the truth contains so much of lying. "For the elegance of simplicity would correctly and squarely presume that having no expectations with regard to the future is inherent to true happiness."

"Yes, but," Andy downs the dregs of the froth, "you have to ask yourself, Wils: Are you a lover or are you a fighter?"

"Neither," I say with a shake of my head. "These days I'm neither."

Having bid farewell to Andy, who, bright and early tomorrow, is flying out to Atlanta, then up to New York, then on to London, then finally to Edinburgh, and rushed home to flip over Matthew, I am changed, still making reasonably good time, and just pulling out of the driveway when I get a call from the boss, who tells me not to report to the office but go straight to a dorm.

It's a dorm we're in the midst of renovating (apparently for decades there's been a major rat infestation, but gutting and refurbishing the dorm, insofar as I can tell, is only going to give a nicer home to the rats, but then nobody's asked my opinion), and there's been an anonymous call that said some kids made their way inside, and one of them went in a chute that went down into the compactor, and when he fell into the compactor the machine turned on and crushed him. So that is where I'm supposed to report.

As I drive to campus, I run through my list of questions, my questions for the scene of an accident. They taught us to think NADA: name, affiliation to the university, date of birth, association to the incident. And then there are the what's, how's, where's, and when's according to relevance. But there won't be any witnesses tonight if we received an anonymous call. And yet it's comforting to know you've got the right questions on hand if you should run into someone with answers.

For a while I was angry—I mean really upset about Becky Jo leaving us in the lurch and not having the decency to help out with Matthew. Then someone recommended I see a therapist, which I decided to do, and now I've got it together. It's imperative, the therapist and I concluded, to live in the present. You can't keep living in the past. Or, for that matter, the future. Just one day at a time. Isn't that what all those gurus say? But I know guys who, finding themselves in my predicament, would instantly take to drink, as an escape. But to me that just seems ludicrous. As if in hammering away at the edge you only show how strong the blade is.

For a while I was having these dreams. We'd be doing something, me and Matthew, some kind of father-son activity. Standing in a sunny lot, playing catch. Or maybe we were in Death Valley, watching the homecoming game. Whatever the incident, everything would suddenly stop. The game would stop; the ball would stop; the sun would stop in the clouds; and everyone would look at us and stare. "You can't take him out! What are you doing?" And then there really was a while when I'd push him in the stroller around the neighborhood or around City Park—more for my benefit, to feel like I was doing something, something that might be right. Now I just adjust the blinds to where the sun won't shine in his face.

I'll never forget, a doctor once told me: "I can do something." "What can you do? We've been everywhere. To dozens of spec—" "No," he said, looking tersely from over his chart. "I mean I know someone who could help you in your situation." And when I still didn't understand: "There's a threshold about what constitutes a Homo sapiens. You ask yourself: Is it in the heart? Is it in the head? Certain desires, a particular set of memories, or perhaps it's a skill or the ability of the mature brain to contemplate itself? Is that what makes a man a man? And you find, in the end, it's nothing, nothing at all in particular. But Matthew, he doesn't have any of that stuff."

The light behind me is starting to return to and fill the sky—I thought about going and saying goodbye to Andy again and even drove to the hotel but then thought the better of it, thought it might seem a little desperate, and then he might ask questions about last night, and that's a whole story in its own right, so I came out to the river, where I'm sitting in an O of BATON ROUGE—the I-10 bridge obscured by fog, the cars speeding over like pale suns passing through a wormhole. Already the morning is humid, and I can hear, among the gravity of the river, the suck and lapping about the levee, which means there must be a barge somewhere cutting the current. I think how nice it would be to have someone there when I come home. A friend like Andy or a wife like Becky Jo or a son not like Matthew. There was a year, a few years after he was born, before Becky Jo walked out, when I told myself: This is your son; you have got to love him; this isn't some kind of choice. And so I pretended that I loved him. Each morning I woke up I told myself: You love your son. I repeated those words while cutting his hair; I repeated those words while clipping his nails, while feeding him with his spoon, while changing his diaper, while taking him to hospitals as we searched for Dr. Miracle. This is someone whom you love, lying there. It doesn't matter, the ocean in his skull, for we are bound by something better. Then after a year of trying to dupe myself, I had to throw in the towel. I was tired of trying to kid myself. My wishful thinking didn't change the fact of that weird croaking; it didn't put a thought in Matthew's brain. All it did was make me want for something more than I could have because it was hardly quite there, and not long after that Becky Jo walked out.

The city smells like gasoline and tar, with a hint of coffee. I think about how new everything used to seem, even when I was a teenager. I think about my first date with Becky Jo, when we were seniors, walking around, taking pictures. Sitting there atop those Indian mounds. I can still remember the February sky. Glass baby blue merging into the white haze on the horizon. Every direction you look. The only time of the year you can still walk around and still get that rush from that subtle cool just lingering in your brain. Had Becky Jo known we'd have Matthew, I'm convinced she never would have married me in the first place. And then I didn't help things by insisting we keep trying. It almost became like a competition, to prove we could do better, that we hadn't failed, to make up for Matthew's dud, and she saw right through all that. I wonder how that girl from Haymarket is, how healthy her kids must be, and how I made a huge mistake after being given the grand opportunity of seeing her again at the chippy.

I think how they were waiting for me at the dorm, Sam and Diego, flanking the compactor like they were eager to introduce us.

"Do we know who it is?"

"No," says Sam. He stomps out a cigarette. Evidently they have been passing between them a flask.

"Mr. Anais is getting footage from the security cameras," says Diego. "Police and ambulance are on their way."

"And the body?"

Diego blinks.

"Body's still inside."

There is a hatch with a lever at the side of the compactor that the elegance of simplicity would infer is a door.

"I'm not going in."

"Prove to me it's turned off."

Diego stands there, flicking the switch. Empty clicking.

"Okay."

"The police'll be here in three minutes."

My foot already partway up, I go, "Last one in's a rotten egg."

The inside of the machine is cool, pitch dark, less humid than the world outside. I imagine my colleagues can see the flicker of my light in the door like the event horizon of who-knows-what-lies-beyond. The smell of paint thinner and asbestos enfumes the air, and the ground is slipshod and springy with the strata of cardboard. I sweep the dark with my flashlight and spot the body lying over in the corner.

The body is first to come out, which I deliver into Sam's and Diego's hands.

"Here."

"Oh my god."

"Yeah."

Then I hoist myself out.

As we are standing around, waiting for the ambulance, none of us can bear to look at that pulverized face and corpse. Once is more than enough. Sam has gathered the boy's wallet, and we now know his name is Michael Thursten. All we can do is try our best not to dissolve into sobs as the sirens grow closer, closer.

I think how Michael Thursten's parents have no idea about what has happened. That they are going about their normal business of sleeping as if the world were right as rain but how this time tomorrow they will not be sleeping once everything has come crashing down, and then I stop myself from pitying these people, telling myself, these hypothetical parents, Well, if you didn't want to be hurt, then you shouldn't have had children. Why did you have children if you didn't want to feel pain? For to engage in this world for even a second is to welcome regret and anguish. Everyone involved is so damn foolish. Michael must have thought he was going down a chute to nowhere.

In the glare of the sirens there is that unmistakable hiccup of fighting down crying. Diego and I look up to find Sam trembling, but in fact he is giggling.

"Look," he points toward the body. "Dumb bastard was walking around all day with his fly down."

The fog now burned away and in its place the condensed thickness of sparrows chirruping and the heady pollen of azalea, honey suckle, and magnolia making the air like a substance in which the city has sunk, and as proof of our collective drowning, no person out on the streets does not appear drenched about the forehead, nose, and armpits, I open the door, which opens unlocked—I thought I had certainly locked it behind me last night, but apparently I did not, don't know when I must have fallen out of the habit—and go to the couch to turn over Matthew and prepare his breakfast of applesauce and whey, but Matthew is not on the couch.

I stop.

Standing before the empty couch, I stay there, watch it, blink. Sooner there is some malfunctioning in the fovea of my eyeballs than Matthew has stirred from that couch. I have not walked in and seen that couch unbodied since the day we bought it twelve years ago. Standing there, blinking, I do the only thing I can think.

"Matthew!" I know my shouting is ludicrous.

I check under the couch—the space is too tight to fit even a pair of slippers, only dust and forgotten coins—walk around the corners of rooms, checking closets, bathtubs, compartments, but there is not a hint of evidence that anyone has been around. Then I return to the back door, study the lock and door very carefully. No one, it seems, has broken in; there is nothing wrong with any of the windows; there is nothing at all to suggest a vandal has been at work. I walk to the front of the house. A woman, pumping her arms, with a bandolier of water bottles is approaching the driveway—I can't tell if she is looking at me from behind her sunglasses, a tan, wiry sack of skin like a stuffed prairie dog on a motor—and I'm about to stop her and ask, "Have you seen my son?" but then realize how insane the whole scene sounds. I go back inside to the cool of the house. People with only brain stems do not simply get up one day and decide to walk away. Nothing of the sort has happened. No, rather, the elegance of simplicity would propound that the child's mother, hounded by grief and remorse, incurred a change of heart and has entered the premises, using the key that opens the lock I have never changed, while I was at work and taken our child. The elegance of simplicity is always reliable.

All that day, whether asleep or awake, I think about Matthew. Part of my subconscious must be mustering up the courage to phone the child's mother and ask her why she has taken him, ask her why she just didn't ask. I would have given him—after some hesitation, to be sure—we could have worked out an agreement to care for him in shifts like normal parents apart—only I would have liked to have been offered that interim of time when I deliberate and consider, when Becky Jo must have to stand by and wait and sweat out the possibility that I may end up turning her down; I would have liked to have been given that opportunity, but the elegance of simplicity does not usually take my personal feelings into account.

Instead, back at the office, I am still toying with the idea of calling her, perhaps waiting to be called myself, since certainly she must know that I know by now that she has come in and taken him. Why not leave me some kind of note? Is it really worth the drama of stealing in and carrying him off in the night, of sending the message I'm not worth corresponding with?

"You brought your report?" says Mr. Anais.

In a frustrating defiance of order, Americans, unlike Brits, do not have faces that lend themselves to an easy division of food-based categories. Naturally I have tried to establish some system—hamburger face, health-shake face, corn-dog face, Hot Pocket face, whatever—but no reliable archetypes emerge, no consistently surfacing patterns. Perhaps our diets are just broader. Rather, the faces of my countrymen dictate their classifications.

"It's right here," I say.

"Good. Shut the door." Mr. Anais gestures. "Have a seat."

For a moment we sit across from each other, not saying anything. It is almost as if neither of us were really here. With perhaps what is curiosity, I study his visage—old and ugly and harried it is and grotesque—a gargoyle face, one worn away by rain but intent to remain ugly all the years, nothing within that flesh to assure me of its dire reality.

"I spoke with Diego and Sam about last night and read their reports, and I've been in touch with the officers who arrived at the scene." He shakes his gargoyle face with what must be incredulousness. "These kids—they come here wanting to learn, and we take them at their word, under the pretense they know how to read, but apparently 'no trespassing' is beyond their vocabulary. I mean, who would think it's a swell idea to go down a blind garbage chute? It's not only tragic, it's downright idiotic." He looks at me as if he has come to the end of his monologue and were waiting for some kind of applause, in lieu of which I offer: "Will there be an investigation?"

"Hell yeah," he says. "We're contacting his roommate at Kirby Smith. The police have already traced the call they made from a Circle K off campus, where hopefully we'll get footage, as in a car with a license plate."

"That's great," I go.

"I guess," says the boss. "Yeah, sure. But you realize you're in a lot of trouble too, though, right?"

"What? Why?" From head to toe all of me goes frozen. "How did I do anything?"

"Because you were as stupid as he was, as in the kid squashed in the trash. What made you think you had any business jumping in there, fishing him out? Why didn't you wait for the cops?"

I cannot look at him or talk. My tongue feels oversized against my teeth. Motor inanition.

"You realize you were breaking protocol? That you were essentially tampering with a crime scene?"

Without meeting his gaze, I can feel his harried glare, know what it looks like without seeing it physically. The framed headlines of sequent baseball victories and famous prints of bouquets and vegetables traveled abroad from museums—they might as soon speak as that person in front of me waiting.

"I . . . I thought . . . we go into cars that get broken into, into dorms with doors staved in. We haul in guys that get mugged. I thought, How is this any different?"

The quiet that passes between us, it is the same species of quiet that haunts the bottom of the ocean, where the manta rays abound and plankton, where the bones of whales get licked clean by sharks; it means that none of this has to be real.

"Here's what's gonna happen: Captain Jameson is gonna put pressure on me to let you go, citing a serious breach in protocol, and he's gonna have the sheriff behind him. But the way I'm going to try to spin this is that you've been here for what—how long?"

"Ten years."

"—ten years, and you're reliable and a good kid and that ultimately you had good intentions, which I'm assuming will be corroborated by your report? Isn't that so?" He looks at me, daring this bubble of ours to pop.

"Yeah," I say. "That's so."

Back at home, having spent the morning phoning up doctors, some of whose receptionists I know better than many of my relatives, and begging them to spare me a second to answer my question, or rather verify my certain knowledge that hydrocephalics do not one day suddenly sprout cerebellums and effect locomotion, that I am generally on the right track about this and not having what seems to be a nervous breakdown, I am now on my last call.

If I try to remember, I cannot recall the ten digits, the code that connects our two points on a planet of at least four dimensions, connects me to Becky Jo. In truth I have no idea whether she's changed her number after all these years, as anyone likely would. If I am to dial it, I must distract myself and attempt to key in the number offhand, as if calling her were a thing as habitual today as it was.

Thus, while picking some lint off the couch, while noticing some of Matthew's stray hairs, the impression of his head, his formless indention across the cushions, somewhere a part of me remembers that combination, even though I could have sworn, gun to my head, that that information lay forever beyond me.

Ringing. Empty ringing is all there is.

"Hello," says a voice. It is the voice of Becky Jo.

"Becky Jo?"

"Wilson!"

It is not quite a greeting so much as a twitch, a jerk, a reaction. Followed by an abrupt stretch of stillness. On days like these I find myself waiting for my heart to stop beating. Won't be surprised any second when it does.

"What's up?"

"Not much," I say, trying to convey unconcern. "And you?"

"Is something the matter?" her voice brightens like a splash in a stream. "Why are you calling?"

"You don't know why I'm calling?" I go, straining to imagine her there by the phone. In my mental image she is standing with her honey-brown hair pinned up in a tight bun and a kind expression that purports she has never known any pain. She is standing in the room of a shotgun shack with several places to sit and pictures on the shelves and walls. Matthew is nowhere to be found. And then I realize that that mental house is mine and those pictures include myself: it is my house I'm imagining, but with her stuff.

"No," she answers coldly.

"You really don't know why I'm calling?"

"No," she repeats just as coldly.

"And there's nothing you want to tell me?"

"No." She takes a breath, which adds emphasis. "I thought we said it's better if we don't have contact? Wilson?"

"I remember. Only . . . one more question: Where are you at these days?"

"What?"

"Where are you living? Are you still in McComb?"

"Why does it matter?"

Her voice sounds cool and certain, as assured of itself as a mathematical law.

"I just want to know." So much for aloofness.

"I don't think that's any of your business."

"It could be my business."

"I'm going to hang up."

"Okay." Then after she doesn't hang up: "What?"

"How's Matthew? Is Mathew okay? Wilson?"

"That depends on how you look at that."

"Keep loving him," she offers. "He knows."

"Okay." The desire is to go off on a tangent about the web of hypocrisy at play here, but such a move would be disastrous, useless.

"Okay. Goodbye, Wilson."

"Goodbye, Becky Jo." We hang up our mutual phones.

Now we are just two people going about on the planet.

Back on the levee, in exactly the same place I was two nights ago after work—I rushed home from work, feigning I was sick, but I was not sick but merely wanting to see, to observe the ocular presence of it, the bare ground, and corroborate the palpable proof of my standing in the empty backyard, that I had not, in a moment of madness, in a fit of irrationality, in a lapse of memory and judgment, in a lacuna of all consequence, carried him to the backyard and left him out in the elements like an offering to the sun, but he is not there, not anywhere in the house or yard, and there was no lacuna, no lapse, no cross-purpose with myself—hearing the great gravitational fall of the river pour its course to the sea, I imagine Matthew's face. The face is too long, oversized, so that anyone who has ever seen it immediately understands something isn't right. As the lips are too thin, as the eyes are too wide, as the skull is too crooked and bent like an abandoned head made of putty. But there is a tranquility to that stark face as well, like a still life faintly pulsing. It lay all day hearing but not knowing what it heard. Seeing but not knowing what it saw. It was the peace of a brain that, when you shined a flashlight against his skull, would light up the other side, making the whole head glow in fleshy radiance. A peace beyond all thought.

Every summer there are stories in the news about kids trying to swim in the river. There are signs up and down the levee warning about the undertow, though the people who end up drowning must never read them. It's a river best admired and let go its way.

I think about that day with Becky Jo on the Indian mounds and the white haze on the horizon, and I hope she is as happy as the world once seemed. I hope the girl from Haymarket is okay too, whatever became of her. I hope the parents of Michael Thursten, who, if they weren't in town, now certainly are, find some comfort as they try to account for their son's lapse in judgment that would make him think going down a blind chute is a good idea.

Unlike two nights ago, tonight you can see clear across to Port Allen and the workers who work on the dock going about in a cloud of brightness, and since it is not yet close to day, only the occasional set of taillights flicker along the I-10 bridge. If I stay here a while, chances are I will get mugged, but I have nothing for them to take. All I have is only a head full of muddled thinking and a dilemma that requires the elegance of simplicity in order to solve.

If my phone call to Becky Jo was proof she failed to sound guilty enough for someone who has unauthorizedly taken a child, and if I myself, as I have just lately established, did not attempt to do something in a fit of unthinking, then the elegance of simplicity would lead me to conclude that the inevitable culprit is Andy, who has come into my house and done something when I was away. Maybe. Which therefore likely means very soon I'll be on a plane to Atlanta, and then on one to New York, and from there on to London, and from London to Edinburgh, to face Andy about what's happened to Matthew. And I know what Andy will say when he sees me standing there on his doormat.

"Well, made it to Auld Reekie have we. Are we a lover now or a fighter?" And I must say what I have to, waiting for Andy to step from my way.

"I'm both."

Let Dogs Delight

ON LOOKING BACK, you perceive patterns, a particular trajectory to a life, and doubt it could have been any way other than what it was. But even in the midst of living can it really be any way else? Are we really so free to step outside ourselves and do something totally radical—as in something beyond the pale of all events and choices that lead us to such a choice?

Her car had run off the road into a pine, killing her instantly. Apart from the tow truck that had disposed of the totaled Mercury and the ambulance that had ferried her remains to the morgue, there had been no bills to pay, no expenses that, had there been a protracted death in a hospital, where machines and medicines and people's livelihoods are involved, would certainly have bled the trust and revived old animosities. Though weeks would pass before anyone uttered the words, her quick death was a blessing, her last act of service in this world.

There was some discussion about scattering the remains in the garden and mixing them with Joy's (she had always said she wanted their dust intermingled), but no one was dressed appropriately, and the notice of death had yet to run in the paper, which might draw out a commiserating acquaintance. Instead, it was decided that Helen would live with Billy and Martha until business could be sorted. There was also some question as to my medication, which Billy reckoned best not taken into account—pleas to the contrary he put down at once. Then, after Helen emerged with her bags, we filed into the van, smells of new places, of new manners and new meals, of new possibilities, and the old bungalow vacant behind me at last. They had forgotten my chattels, but what did I care, for where I was going was an improvement.

    I had never been to the Stadlers—that is, to the Stadlers in Baton Rouge; Joy had, on multiple occasions (those were the years before relations had become more frayed by Bill's demise), and had relayed information and judged the place ideal—though I had abandoned all hope of seeing it, as Joy had of going back by the time we were introduced. She had come in, happy and good-natured despite the cast on her leg, but the years had taken their toll—not that she was resentful or had succumbed to pessimism or self-pity, rather, I suppose, she had come to welcome her situation as anyone would, eventually taking the chains and shackles for ornaments and adornments, the deprivation of which would constitute a sort of nudity, not so much shameful as uncomfortable. She had leaned into her captivity without any thought of escape.

    At first we got along well, like siblings; she was helpful at filling with details the adumbrations of sighs, of mutterings in the hall, of insinuations and allusions to people and incidents unknown to me while I struggled to make sense of my situation. But within the year I no longer had any feelings for her, and began to think of her, if at all, more as a fixture, like a moveable piece of furniture, than as a friend or potential mate, and her blithe dedication and her suffering herself to be so handled served to put me off, so that I determined, if not to become inured to the difficulty of my circumstances or complacent to the extent of being grateful simply for having a roof over my head, to derive benefit from a practice of lethargy instead of ingratiating myself to someone who struck me as fundamentally impossible. Even during those trips across the lake to the barn, where we would go for the pleasure of "watching Crickets" (since Crickets had been deemed unrideable), I would lie away in the shade of a tractor or trailer, ignoring the wisecracks of the bumpkins whose jests were mainly overtures to induce me to tell them about city life (as though Metairie were so urbane) and perhaps on some level hoping the tractor would suddenly reverse with the same effect as the Grand Marquis had had that day on Joy, only, in my case, to break my neck.

It was at the barn that Elise met Joy. Elise, by that point, was forty. She had always been a nervous driver, especially if the errand was not to her liking; then you could be sure we would be riding to a fanfare of honking. There had been some discussion about her social security (or lack of it), which had led to her fleeing the scene, bags packed and everything, no matter that she could not count a cent to her name, and she had cut out for the barn, I take it, to make whatever plans she could for Gypsy. In her haste she had reversed too quickly and a bright squeal, that tocsin that was to eradicate her plans of breaking away, went up. Or perhaps nothing would have changed. Elise leapt from the car and found her with a broken leg. "Oh no!" she said in that inveterate singsong, that cartoon of child's pain. "Ooo, I'm so sorry! I should have been paying attention!" She was panting from the agony, yet her eyes were big and hopeful. "I'm sure you had a lot on your mind. That you weren't looking is understandable. But, crikey, could you bring me, please, to a doctor?" Which was how she became a fixture, as I say, around the house. Bill could hardly protest—he did protest (that is, when he was not raving about Falaise pockets and the dark forest at Buchenwald), but in light of the fact he was bedbound, a silhouette spraddled in front of the television, his voice a declarative whisper as a result of the congestive heart failure that would carry him off by the end of the year—and he must have soon realized that expelling Joy from his house was as likely as his recovery. Things worked there by way of acquiescence, a bowing to the sheers of fate. Thus was hers spun and measured.

She would nurse Bill to the end, and now she had Joy to look after. The more she could help, the happier she was. Along with her nature to be put to incessant use, there was a predilection for surrounding herself with objects needing repair. As a girl she had taken in sparrows who had run into the window and incurred broken wings, a baby squirrel who had fallen and hurt its back, turtles with split shells who had been hit along the canal—there had been a predecessor, many years before, whose scent still lingered on unworn clothing, not a shepherd like Joy but some parvenu spaniel whom she had taken to sketching in various attitudes and habiliments, whose curious semblances peered, sometimes quizzically, sometimes with a sentiment akin to tenderness, an evident vulnerability, as if Elise had not only detected but managed to capture that indelible cry for help, as if mistaking pathos for pitifulness, down at us from the walls—and during her year away at school she had adopted a parakeet who was confiscated in due course, but she was always freest while on a horse. She would ride for hours, trotting the perimeter of the pasture, oblivious to everything save bounding there in the saddle. The day was fine; the horse was sweating and smelling of dust and the vitality of its leather. In the distance came the sound of hammers fastening a new steel roof on the barn, and she would turn to the horse or Billy and savor them with something of the fondness of a bride waking up on her first morning as a married woman, with the pure insouciance that all the years ahead will be as such. Years later—after her failure to make something of herself at college—it was precisely this that Bill realized he could turn to his advantage, could throw into the bargain to ensure he could continue taking those trips to Florida, away from Elise, away from Helen, away from the decisions and acquiescences that had led him to himself: her remaining at the house was contingent on her caring for Helen, but, in the exchange, she would get her horse. That was the price of her freedom.

The fixation on riding had started not long after Helen returned from Meadowood. On weekend mornings, while his wife lay on the couch, Bill would ferry the three of them to the country, where they took lessons in dressage and learned how to groom a stable of purebred horses. In fact, Billy had been the one to suggest it: whatever he did, wherever he went, his little sister was always dogging him, doing as he did, until he eventually tired of her and ran her off, or lost interest in the activity himself.

For instance, one weekend they were playing around the uncovered cesspool. If Elise didn't leave, Billy said, he would push her into the pool. She told him they had to play together. Billy repeated his threat. She said he'd better not, and forced him to swear, to which Billy stuck out his hand, but when she went to clasp it, he jerked back his hand, which caused her to fall in the pit. The other boys laughed, and the pack of them ran off. I can imagine her there, covered in mire. I can picture her beseeching some ordering justice to the world to smite Billy down and torture him for his meanness. I say that I can imagine Elise indulging in this wishful thinking because I myself, at least for the first few years, was as prone to it as she—however, unlike Elise, I ultimately concluded that such thinking is futile, that any clinging to the hope of some miraculous intervention is not only folly, is fundamentally useless, and very likely a socially acceptable display of madness, but that hope is no virtue at all but the mind vainly deluding itself. For you imagine not some minor personal grievance such as this but a catastrophe beyond comprehension—for example, those frightened people being crammed into the showers time after time and praying for a miracle, anything, for the walls to cave in, for an earthquake to cleave the floor, for a divine army to come down and save the day—and that no governing order intervened must lead one to conclude that God is not intercessory. And if God is not going to shape events to one's dire wanting, then it necessarily accords that events must be hoped to be brought about by oneself. Yet Elise, I am certain, never took this lesson to heart. Of all the Stadlers, only Bill seems to have fathomed it to the root of his principles, and not, of course, as a young man, and likely not still as a young husband and father, but only after years of waiting for that inert woman on the couch to get better, to improve, to delight him as she once had in the happy spring of their courtship, could he have understood the fruitlessness of hope.

He would come back after a long day at the office and try not to be annoyed that they were eating hot dogs and applesauce for a fourth night in a row. If the kids were causing trouble, he was usually quick to yell. Punishing them came not from a place of despising them; he just wanted life to be a little easier than it was. Then she broke the bottle. I imagine there was some petty annoyance—perhaps he could not bring himself to ingest another hot dog, or perhaps there was evidence she had been letting the kids run amok—and he let go some quip or carp, but whatever it was, she took up the ketchup bottle and broke it against his head. For that she stayed two months in Mandeville. Hence the riding, hence the perennial fighting of brother and sister, hence Bill's trips to Florida alone. When Helen came back she was a shadow of herself, the couch her permanent residence . . . sprawled there, silent, inert.

Then Billy left for college. In spite of the fact he had become almost an enemy, to Elise it felt like a betrayal, as though he had gone off with his friends and found a hiding place where she was forbidden to enter. Two years later she followed him to the capital. She left, thinking she had outwitted him at last, discovered the password to his fort, but by then he was in love and wanted nothing even more to do with her. The city was a bigger place to hide than the neighborhood. As a result she sat in her room and began to yearn to be back in Metairie—the old resentments, the old reminders, none of it seemed so hurtful from the perspective of eighty miles. So she left school and fell back into the routine of caring for Helen as Bill approached his retirement. Not long afterward Billy married; then they were expecting a baby, and Elise convinced Bill to let her get Gypsy. As I said, Elise was entirely mortified to operate a car—she felt like a swimmer going after some object, mindful it is only blind will keeping afloat life and will—but was willing to endure that terror for the sake of something she wanted, and I believe that had either Bill or Billy been there in the passenger's seat by her side, she would have felt she was in good hands, but that something about the freedom of the road, her utter lack of faith in her abilities to control a multi-ton machine, and her distrust of the alacrity of others served to curarize her to the bone. Nevertheless, she would visit Gypsy two to three times a week, making that journey across the lake, those twenty or so miles without any shoulder to pull over on should she incur a blowout or require a break to stop and catch her breath.

Even after Bill died and Gypsy, whom Elise had decided to breed, died while giving birth, and she was driving to the barn almost daily to spend the night nursing the foal, the driving never got any easier. Joy would be there, sitting beside her, Elise watching the road and daring to look over now and then, and Joy trained on Elise, quelling her fear. "You're doing great. Just keep your eyes on the road and a light tap of the brake, and that's all there is. Ripper, you're a natural!" In those terrible drives to the barn, Joy was almost a parent; she helped tidy the brutal disquiet of her mind, and it was on just such a drive that I was spotted. I do not say "I was found," although I had no idea where I was going, only that, being the runt of the litter, I knew I would have to make my way in the world and, whether that was to become dinner for a hawk, the flattened result of a driver distracted on the phone, or an inhabitant of the swamps who preyed on garbage, I was prepared to let fate take the wheel—and that thick mane of hair came down and scooped me up.

The house smelled of sugar cookies and vaguely of potpourri. From the outset I knew that I had done better than had I been left to scavenge among the cast-off tires and cypress knees; additionally, I realized in due course that in forgoing the instant gratification of a subpar meal I could come to expect the same comestibles of which the others partook, which, though mediocre in their own right (indeed, there seemed to be an outright aversion to herbs and spices), proved the lesser evil, a practice that Joy never cared to espouse or condoned and that, I suspect, has led to my present issue with ulcers. But then, after I gained a sense of my new environment and on what and whom I could rely, there were practices in which Joy engaged that forced me to make my disapproval evident as well: there were, for example, those long accompaniments to the washroom, those constant consolations and affirmations that even a four-year-old would have interpreted as pure condescension, and the pretense of protection for this family who, I could never make Joy agree, needed more protection from themselves if there were ever a knock at the door—not to mention the two of them on the bed. Even during the last night, she was still going up, not so much out of service, of performing a duty, but simply because she wished, was glad to be used in such a manner, as if in Elise's will should be her peace. Did they make love, you're wondering? That depends on how you define such a thing. We are told that one may make love in the mind's eye; conversely, that means that one may make love without ever really making love at all. So perhaps your question should be: Did Elise believe she was making love? And the answer to that, I think, would probably be yes and no—which is to confirm that all her romantic feelings merely adapted to the means at hand. For instance, I recall there was a remark she let drop when the seven of us were on vacation regarding something about giving William a banana sling, a comment she soon followed by entrusting to him her Aunt Elise's wedding ring, which I am certain he immediately hocked. With her there was always this ill-suited need to be of service, to be helping, to be of use, just as I observed in Billy a similar trait, that he was possessed by an indelible urge to syllogize, traits, I assume, they inherited from the silences of their childhood, alone with that woman who, if she was not sleeping all day on the couch, would read her prayer book cover to cover.

 She was talking right to the end, when she and Joy were forced to say goodbye, when anyone would beg for a moment's silence to compose their thoughts; she was slobbering all over Joy, who, once more, was paying for it in the role of caregiver (I gave Joy the gift of my peace, though it had been years since we were on speaking terms). "I'm so sorry!" "Don't ever say you're sorry. You made me a better dog." It was bone cancer; the cancer was in the leg opposite the one Elise had run over; hence, there was no way of saving her, of removing the leg and her remaining mobile, contrary to Elise's wishful thinking. "You can't take care of a dog without hind legs!" the doctor had tried to explain to her. The two of us watched Joy led away and heeling faultlessly alongside the nurse. As for me, I did not wish to console Elise. To lick those tears, at that point in my thinking, would have been anathema to my principles, and perhaps just as misguidedly I believed that, like the collar the nurse returned at the end of our wait, a shackle had been cast off. Perhaps now she will run away, I thought; the two of us will go across the lake and check into a Ramada, and in a few weeks she will be leading trail rides along the swamp, and eventually she will make enough in order to collect the social security that she will need to survive. Instead, she piled on the manacles. She began to amass antiques, stuff she convinced herself had been overlooked by the rest of the world as to its value, and she was hoarding her trove for the great day of reckoning when she would cash in on her perspicacity, one of these items being an enormous tapestry, a reproduction, nearly the size of a billboard, of the Cluny unicorn, which she thrust on Bill on his wedding day, that furled and cumbersome symbol of chastity in tote throughout the drive halfway across the country with Billy and Martha, who must have surely been bridling their annoyance, as if she insisted on bearing with her the stigma of her fantasy or the impossible sign of her life's clutter, a magical horse that can never be found, let alone ridden, save in a dream.

"Leave!" I'd tell her. "What are you waiting for? You don't have to stay. Let Billy and Martha take care of her. At worst they'll throw her in some upscale facility." But somewhere in who she was she had long ago made up her mind never to change or believe there was an option or opportunity for things to be different (perhaps, on considering the possibility, feeling a dread akin to the terror she had felt that night Helen had broken the bottle over Bill's head, the sight of her father's blood barely distinguishable from the travesty of the condiment splattered over him and the tablecloth), and she was unable even to begin to offer an account of herself, her situation. Those regular calls from Billy, whom she plainly resented on account of his having a family of his own, for his having severed himself insofar as to live eighty miles away to the north, who worried how she would survive, on her own, without a job, after Helen died—even those caustic shouting matches did not so much succeed in spurring her to look for a new kind of work with their wild prognostication of a reality soon to be as enflame her wrath, her resentment. "I do not have a problem! And we are doing just fine, thank you! And Dad, by the way, was a jerk!" The question was always: How would she live once the trust was depleted? She was not entitled to social security—she had never worked for any real business a day in her life, only ferried Helen to appointments and made sure her whims were attended to—and the trust would be gone in ten years: Elise by then would be seventy and would need caring for herself. Everyone said prayers. Me, I did not pray; it was obvious she was not going to change and enjoyed her captivity far more than she would have ever savored her freedom—or rather, she had found a particular freedom under which any radical uprooting would have suddenly exposed new, more unseverable bonds, and she dreaded their revelation.

Then an idea was proposed: Billy had called the lawyer and there was a paperwork possibility they could declare Elise to be an employee of the trust, which might bring her a pittance of social security—it would be expensive, and some figures would have to be altered, but apart from her coming to live with Billy and Martha (an option that I alone entertained), it looked like the sole way ahead.

A meeting with the lawyer was scheduled. I knew she would take issue with the arrangement, despite that all she had to do was sign and date her name, and then she would become the government's headache and not the burden of her kin. All that morning I watched her pace back and forth, talking to herself, her well-preserved face, whose agerasia made her appear less like a person her age and more like an old lady wearing a child's mask, frowning, trembling, whimpering, and I knew she would never abide a simple solution. "Ooo, Georgie. I just can't do it." "Sure you can," I said, not really paying much attention but watching some schnauzer roam between the mailboxes, sniffing each by each. "Just put your paw on the papers and scrawl your name. You can do that, can't you?" She was saying the same thing the whole way to the lawyers. "I'm sorry . . . I just can't do it." "Do it!" I barked. And that's when we ran off the road. It is possible we hit an oil slick—I am positive that no one ran us off, and the tire blew out, I am sure, after we went off the shoulder—and, I suppose, there is also the explanation, however remote, that a coincidental malfunction forced the steering a hard right, but whatever the case, that's when we hit the tree. The window was cracked, but had not shattered; thus I was trapped and waiting to be let out, though had there been some means by which to break free and reside in the swamps, avoiding the roads, where someone might identify me on account of my collar, I don't think I would have done it. Firstly, I knew I would not be returning to that house, at least not for long, since Helen was fundamentally incompetent at providing for me by herself, which meant the likelihood I would move in with Billy and Martha. Secondly, being the far side of middle-aged, the thought of scavenging for trash and hoping I might be so lucky as to alight from time to time on a nest of baby nutria rats did not seem as appealing as the prospect once had. And thirdly, the wreck had accentuated the pain in my stomach, thereby forcing me to sit and wait. And wait I did. Nevertheless, during those hours I spent in the car, I began once again to reflect on those poor people who were trapped in the showers with no chance of escape and who were likely praying with all their hearts for some divine intervention, and never got any, and how I had not only approached the whole issue wrong but inferred a mistaken conclusion: rather than concluding that God was not intercessory, which thereby gave license to my gluttony, lethargy, and years of idle self-licking, I should have concluded that there was no ultimate conclusion that one could hope to afford in the face of these events, that, when presented with them, all thinking, all words, all logic, and therefore all judgment, seemed, as it were, to roll over, and that the only way of proceeding would have to be one not so much unreliant on God as unreliant on any wanting to shape events, which thereby rendered me a sort of delightful disinterest in what moments now were left to me, so that what I suddenly felt while waiting through those hours was joy—pure, intenerate joy: joy to be where I was, joy to be who I was, joy at what would be. I could have gone on waiting like that forever.

Eventually arrived the police, and then the ambulance. Then Billy and Martha. Then the next day came Bill and Meredith. And the next day Elise returned, this time in a condition the size of a jewelry box and smelling remotely of herself, as if she had rolled around in last year's leaves.

When we got out of the car, I recognized the place at once. On our way to Baton Rouge we had made a pit stop at the doctor's, the same place where, years earlier, I had watched Joy say goodbye to Elise. Billy led me in while the rest of them stayed in the car, and behind me I could feel that autonomous metronome suddenly spring to life and begin to thrash, keeping sporadic time. So long had it been since the last time I felt it whip I gave a sudden start, but my fright was quickly dispelled, for I recalled it signified I was happy. I was on my way to new experiences, to live with the family I had never let myself dream of having. I was happy at last, for I was on my way to my home.

Hitler in Love

WE WERE OUTSIDE by the playground when they came running through the gate. At first there were only a few, but by the time they reached us, the whole building was out and running, and someone had pulled the fire alarm. A few explosions had already gone off, but none of us gave them any thought. The morning had been the first cold one, and by the afternoon the temperature had not gotten any warmer.

The cool girls were standing in a circle while I sat reading by the fence. I pretended to ignore them whenever they talked about me. At some point we heard explosions and not long after that the sirens. That's when they came running.

Chanie was the first to reach us.

"Aren't you supposed to be in Algebra?" said Maya. "Why aren't you in Mrs. Kaufman's? Hey, what's going on?"

She looked like she wanted to cry or say something, but she couldn't make up her mind which.

"What?" said Maya.

Then the whole building was out running toward us. I saw Mrs. Kaufman holding the door. She looked wild there, screaming and holding the door and pointing.

I'm sure someone else told us before Chanie said anything.

"Someone's shooting the school."

They had us packed in the gymnasium. There were so many of us we had to sit around on the floor. If someone wanted to come down from the top of the bleachers, he could forget about it; moving was impossible. For the whole time we were crammed in, we were listening to sirens. Police were guarding the door. Some of us were crying while others were taking the opportunity to hang out and talk with friends. Not everyone was even one hundred percent sure that someone was shooting the school. A lot thought maybe a science experiment had gone wrong, which was what had set off the fire alarm, and maybe I would have thought that too if all the teachers hadn't looked so fearful. After a while the noise of everyone talking made it easy to sit and read.

Then Rabbi Gelley came in with a policeman. He held up his hands, trying to clear a path, but there was no room for them to move forward. Eventually someone had the good idea of sitting in each other's laps. That cleared some room, and they were able to go ahead.

"You have all been very patient," said the policeman once we were silent, "which has made it easy—or as easy as possible—for us to do our job. We are just about to release you. However, before we do, Rabbi Gelley has asked us to say an official word. At one-thirty today an active shooter entered your school. Using an assault rifle, he was able to get past security and enter the Groner Building, where he started, it looks like, firing shots at random. Along the way he killed a security guard and injured another, who pushed the panic button. The shooter also . . . and it is with great sadness that I have to inform you . . . the shooter also shot and killed a student. After which he shot himself."

Outside it was crazy. They let us out into the breezeway, and behind the gate pressed up were camera crews, news reporters I recognized from TV. People were screaming at us for a word. In the time we'd been inside it had started to rain. Parents were crying and fighting to get through the barricade.

As the police were leading us out, we saw yellow tape over the entry to the Groner Building. The building had the look of something that had changed, of something that had become wrong. I searched along the concrete for signs of blood or bullet holes, but there was only yellow tape.

"Oh, my baby!"

It took me a second to realize that the person who'd grabbed me was Imma.

"My baby!"

Some of her tears were wiping off on my cheeks, making it look like I was crying.

For the rest of the evening the phone rang. Friends and relatives from all over the world called as soon as they heard the news. Abba had come home early from a trip and had been given special permission to use his cell phone on the plane. In the middle of all the craziness they'd forgotten to call Ms. Schreiber, who came over at her usual time. Later Imma said she must have been checking to be sure that I wasn't the one who was dead, since that would mean she wouldn't make this month's rent.

"And how was your Rosh Hashanah?" said Ms. Schreiber.

Imma was in the other room on the phone, and the TV was blaring, which made it difficult to be able to concentrate.

"You did tashlikh. And did you enjoy your apples and honey? What little girl doesn't like apples and honey?"

I was trying to think how to answer when Imma came in. She was off the phone. Her face was red and puffy from yelling and crying for so long.

"How horrible! What a nightmare, an absolute nightmare. I never thought that something like this would be happening to me." She came over and gave me another big hug and began to straighten my hair while Ms. Schreiber looked on, pleased. "Some days I think I'm cursed."

"We must count our blessings," said Ms. Schreiber.

"Oh, Morah, if you only knew. It isn't enough that—"

Then the phone rang again, and Imma hurried off to answer it while the two of us sat on the bench.

"Yes, she's doing fine," she was telling whomever had called. "She was on the playground! I know, it's absolutely horrible! I don't know what else to keep saying! I've prayed a thousand times that something like this would never happen, but I guess it wasn't enough. The whole world's become a nightmare, an absolute, total nightmare. If our parents had only grasped what lay ahead, they would never have crossed the Atlantic—or, who knows, maybe never had children."

I played a couple chords.

"What's that?" said Ms. Schreiber offhand but slightly interested.

I kept on playing, what I could remember.

"I've heard that somewhere."

She was chewing her tongue to keep her still listening. She looked angry because she was confused.

When I ran out of what I knew, I said, "Mendelssohn."

"That's right, the second concerto." She played the bars I'd just played, then a little bit more, and where she finished she began to hum. Then she abruptly stopped.

"Yes, rapturous, but ultimately shallow through and through. Which is always what Mendelssohn's problem is. He was always David's most favorite. Hopefully that hasn't rubbed off on you. Another of those self-hating Jews among the likes of Mahler, Rubinstein, and Schoenberg. Unlike Moszkowski. Now Moszkowski—there's a man to cleave to your heart."

The phone continued to ring for the rest of the evening, all through dinner, through the birkat hamazon, until Abba unplugged the cord so I wouldn't be disturbed as I was trying to fall asleep. The way he and Imma kept looking at me, it made me feel punished, like I had done something, but nobody wanted to say what it was.

Imma had been crying when they came in to tell me goodnight. She stayed a while beside me, running her fingers through my hair, until she fell asleep; then she woke and got up to go out, creeping very darkly through the door like a monster troubled by its thoughts.

"I'm at my nerves' end," Imma was saying in the living room. "I won't be able to sleep now for weeks. I haven't even begun to start processing it all. My nerves are still in shock."

I could tell Abba was writing while he listened to Imma.

"Dena says the school is still going forward with opening tomorrow, in spite of everything. I don't agree. I don't know whose idea or decision it was or what they think they're trying to prove. Do you think we ought to hold her back? Tomorrow seems far too soon. I'm thinking we should keep her at home, or better, we should transfer her."

"Transfer her?" said Abba. The scratching had stopped.

"Yes, transfer her. To some place we know is safe, where something like this won't ever happen—to Herschel or the Reform school—anywhere just so long as it's where we know she'll be absolutely safe. Are you listening to me, Yossi?"

"I'm listening."

"Well?"

I could hear him arranging his papers and put the cap back on his pen.

"We're not transferring her, and tomorrow we're sending her back. As a symbolic act of solidarity."

"Yes, that's all well and good of you to say such a nice, lovely thing, but I don't want a symbolic act of solidarity to be the reason—"

"Kucher is as safe as anywhere. Their security's the best in the city, which we said when we decided on schools three years ago, remember? And besides, Kucher will have security out the wazoo after today. It will be the safest place on the planet."

"But, Yossi . . . if that had been my baby."

"Do we know whose it was?"

"We don't have a clue. I've been on the phone all evening with half the entire school, and no one can tell me anything, not a word. It's an absolute, utter mystery. Everyone says they know nothing. How can they know nothing? They're practically all cousins."

"We have to have a sense of hakarat HaTov as we grapple with this. We have to—"

"But, Yossi, if that had been *my baby*. If that had been *my baby* . . . I'd be as good as dead." I could hear her starting to cry.

"But it wasn't."

"It isn't enough, whatever the level of security, to protect us from all these wackos."

There was quiet as the two of them sat in the living room. Then Abba cleared his throat.

"Has David phoned?"

"It's seven hours ahead there, Yossi. I'm sure he's sound asleep."

"No. I'm sure he's very much awake," said Abba.

The yellow tape had been removed, but there were still plenty of police everywhere carrying great black mean-looking guns and patrolling the grounds in loops, and there were still a handful of reporters hanging around in the parking lot, which made it harder to tell that the school was dead since a majority of the students had not shown up. Even several teachers had called out. Ms. Ferber, we heard, had quit.

As a result of all the confusion, they let us have twice the normal amount of recess.

I sat by the gate, rereading the assignment for fifth hour while the cool girls stood in a circle. No one was running around or playing. Everyone, even the younger school, was just standing around, talking in whispers.

"My mother said she's transferring me," said Audrey. "I'll only be here till the end of the month."

"My parents are saying that too," said Andrée.

"But that isn't enough time to get credit for the semester!" said Maya. "You'll have to repeat the whole year!"

"No, I won't. Rabbi Gelley will tell them to give me full credit. He went to yeshiva with my dad, and he'll do anything my dad tells him to do."

"Does anyone know who the student was?" said Esther.

No, said everyone. Everyone looked around to see if anyone hadn't answered.

After an awkward silence Rivkie spoke up. "I know who it is." In class she was always the first to raise her hand, even if more often than not she was wrong. She just liked thinking she was intelligent, even if she only came off as rash.

Who is it? Who?

"It's Alvie Pincus. He was the one who was shot."

"Who's that?" said Esther.

"You know, Alvie Pincus," said Rivkie. "He came here for the first time this semester from somewhere up north."

"I always thought he was weird," said Maya.

"My mom has a friend who's friends with his mother, and that's how she found out."

"He was actually a really big nerd. Nobody liked him."

"It's actually really sad."

"He actually had a really huge crush on Adina!" said Maya, suddenly pointing to me. "He told me one day he'd marry her!"

I'd glanced up from my book.

"Yeah, Noam told me he told him, and I asked him and he said yes. He said he thought you were the most beautiful girl he'd ever laid eyes on, and he was hoping you'd say yes when it came time to marrying him one day. But I guess you can forget about that now. What, you don't believe me?"

I could only keep staring.

"Look, she doesn't believe me."

"That's because she's dumb."

"And fat."

"You know her mother still makes her bathe her."

"Hey, cut it out," said Esther. "You're not being nice. She's actually really smart."

"Now she'll never be married, poor thing," said Maya, batting her eyes toward the clouds like she always did, theatrically. "Now she'll be all alone, with hairs on her chin like my aunt."

Alvie Pincus. We had only ever looked at each other. I went through my memories, trying to find out the one where I should have known, the clue behind the mystery of what had just been revealed, but from all I was able to remember, he'd acted like everyone else, with no hint for me to tell. And now it had passed. Would be that way forever.

Alvie Pincus. He'd barely been here a month, and already he'd made a reputation for himself as one of the most hated kids in school. Word had spread how he and Ms. Ferber had had it out that day in class. The project had been on Great Men of the Twentieth Century, and the whole class had gone up in flames when he'd presented his report.

"My report is on Adolf Hitler."

All of us went cold.

"What?" said Ms. Feber. "This isn't for joking."

"I'm not joking, Ms. Feber. I couldn't think of a better person to do it on than Hitler."

"But no. No, no, Alvie. You misunderstood the assignment. The assignment was on *great* men. And Adolf Hitler is most definitely *not* great. In fact, he's far the opposite. I'm afraid this is unacceptable. You're going to have to rethink it."

"But this *is* the assignment. You said 'great,' and the way I interpreted it was *great* as in very powerful. As in influencing a lot of history. And if you look at it that way, then you'll see he was definitely great."

"No, Alvie. I mean *great* as in he was great."

He'd presented his report, and as a result he'd been given an F and nobody liked him.

By the end of the day everyone was saying how brave Alvie had been. The school was going to put up a special memorial for him and the security guard who'd been killed, and someone had said there was talk of renaming a wing of the Groner Building, the building where he'd been shot, after him. Now everyone had been his best friend; now everyone had plenty of stories that attested to their friendship. But no one was able to say how he'd been hoping one day to marry them. No one could say they had had a future with Alvie Pincus.

At home Imma had already heard. It was all she talked about.

"His father transferred here over the summer. They're Masortis from New York. Apparently quite well-to-do."

"Mmm," agreed Abba. He was writing notes on his proofs in the margins, focusing under the lamp.

"And what's more, what makes matters worse, is apparently the family had been giving to Kucher ever since the beginning, with connections on the board. And now when they finally have a child invested in the institution . . . The situation is very sad, to say the least."

"It *is* very sad."

"Dena said they're delaying the levaya to give the relatives time to travel. She knows a lady who's part of the chevra kadisha. Which'll put it on Erev Yom Kippur. Can they do that, Yossi?"

"What, delay the levaya?"

"That and Erev Yom Kippur."

"They shouldn't, but who can blame them? So long as the levaya is before midday, no one will make a big stink." He was biting the tip of his eraser like it was some private object that might stop the noise.

"Half the family has made aliyah, according to Dena."

"Motek, please. I'm trying to finish my work."

"He's trying to finish his work," Imma said to me. I was doing my homework on the floor by the sofa. "Your father gets fussy when you interrupt him when he's trying to finish his work. It'll be up to you one day to make aliyah. Abba and I are deep in our second mortgage. Do you want to make aliyah one day?" I nodded. "Good. That's a very good girl." She motioned for me to come over so she could rebraid my hair.

"Need I remind you that one of us has made aliyah?" said Abba, not looking up.

"Yes, Yossi, but it's not enough if they're not practicing."

The service was held the next day. The entire school turned out. There were so many of us that people had started to park at the Cabela's across the street and were racing their families across the highway. I recognized reporters and several camera crews who'd been waiting outside the barricade that day of the shooting, only here they stood at the door as groups of us walked in. Along with the nods and handshakes many were quick to laugh since the day was a good excuse to be with friends.

Rabbi Gelley got up and said a few words, thanking everybody for coming out and their support. He promised we'd somehow get through everything and that love in the end would triumph. I looked around. His wife was already in tears. All of us were thinking about poor little Alvie Pincus. All of us were saddened by the unexpected loss.

As we followed behind the coffin, I spotted Mr. Pincus holding his wife's thin hand. From the way she was stooped, I could tell she must have been crying, and I could tell he was making her keep going, or else she would have stopped. Between them you could see the resemblance. If it weren't for him, everything might have ground to a halt, but the firmness of his hand insisted we keep moving forward.

I looked to the right and to the left. Everyone was walking close beside someone else, and if they weren't, they were walking in similar groups. Some of them, like Mr. and Mrs. Pincus, were following, holding on to each other, while others had come as part of another gathering, all of us moving along and wandering after each other as in a parade of people after-dreaming. I searched for

Abba and Imma, and when I turned I saw they had been behind me the whole time, holding on to me, but it had felt like they were somewhere else in the crowd.

As we stood by the grave, people were taking turns taking the shovel and shoveling in dirt. In spite of the hundreds of us packed around where we'd laid him and standing among the gravestones, I could have been anywhere. At the store or in the airport. Among so many bodies that seemed to emit no heat. Maybe a handful of people, I thought, would have come to my grave if I were the one who'd been shot. Either way, it was me and everyone else.

The only way, I thought, for everything to go back to normal was if Alvie were still alive. If it had been Rivkie or Maya or Mrs. Kaufman who'd been out walking in the hall, that would have left alive Alvie, and there'd be time for him to declare his love. He'd be at the funeral, only standing here beside me. But as it was, I was by myself. I thought: I am a widow before I ever became a wife.

I closed my eyes and prayed to HaShem to make Alvie still alive, to make it somebody else who'd been shot, to make everything still okay, and clasped my hands and imagined that one of the hands holding the other would transform into Alvie's, that I'd look up and there he'd be. I squeezed down as hard as I could to where it might have been someone's hand, but when I opened my eyes and the sight realigned, nothing whatsoever had changed. We were all still right where we were. The same people were standing together; the same people still were crying.

At last we parted into sides, and Mr. and Mrs. Pincus, followed by the relatives, filed out as everyone wished them well. "HaMakom yenakhem etkhem," said one person ... then another ... then another, as the bereaved passed by through the opening. "HaMakom yenakhem etkhem." I closed my eyes and imagined they were saying the words to me.

"HaMakom yenakhem etkhem."

"HaMakom yenakhem etkhem."

Even once we were home and that afternoon and then later through dinner, benching, and going to bed, I caught myself saying it almost in my head, "HaMakom yenakhem etkhem." I must have said it dozens of times before I realized what I'd been saying.

"Oh, Yossi. It's just so horrible. Did you see the parents? Did you see the way they looked? Those poor people, how composed they were! I don't understand how they could bear such a thing. If that had been my baby, I wouldn't have shown my face. I'd follow her to the grave. How do you think they could look so . . . *composed*? And to think, that poor woman, Mrs. Pincus—Shifra said she hasn't eaten anything in days. Whatever she's had, I'm sure it isn't enough for her to continue fasting for another day longer. My heart goes out to them, very truly."

I could feel Abba nodding, sitting there under the lamp with his papers, quietly, softly agreeing.

I wondered about Alvie, cold in his grave, and what it must be like to be trapped in such a place, with no hope of ever soon escaping, and how it was okay because being dead meant never knowing that you were. I thought about poor Mrs. Pincus, who was also lying in the dark somewhere, but how she was alive and how she had Mr. Pincus to tell her she was all right, because the two of them were alive. I thought about Alvie, and I thought about Hitler. How Hitler had been really terrible and how no one, no matter how hard they ever tried, could be any worse than Hitler, even if they spent their whole lives doing terrible, horrible things like murdering lots of people and killing innocent babies, that chances were someone would put a stop to them before they ever began to catch up, and how, according to Alvie's report, Hitler had had a wife. Hitler had had someone who had loved him. Someone who, in spite of everything, in spite of Hitler's absolute worst horribleness, had told him that they still loved him, who stayed with him through thick and through thin, and in that case chances were that if Hitler had found somebody, then odds were maybe I would find somebody too. Which meant he was very likely out there some place in the world right now this second. He was living, breathing, sleeping—maybe wondering about me too. This person who would one day marry me and tell me he loved me, that I was his everything, that I was enough for him, enough and so much more. He would tell me he had loved me back then, had always loved me, just as he did now. Just as he always would.

Author Photo © Marion Ettlinger

Devin Jacobsen is the author of the novel *Breath Like the Wind at Dawn* (Sagging Meniscus, 2020). He was born and grew up in Baton Rouge, Louisiana. He currently lives in Paris.